mvpkids

DNA CHRONICLES™

To the New World and Back™

SOPHIA DAY®

Written By **Carol Sauder**

Illustrated by **Stephanie Strouse**

mvpkids

The Sophia Day® Creative Team - Carol Sauder, Stephanie Strouse, Megan Johnson, Kayla Pearson, Timothy Zowada, Mel Sauder

A special thank you to our team of reviewers who graciously give us feedback and edits and who help ensure that our products remain accurate, applicable, and genuinely diverse.

Library of Congress Cataloging in-Publication Data
Day, Sophia.
To the New World and Back™.
Summary: Blake goes back in time to 1620 and sees life through the eyes of his ancestor. He experiences firsthand the riveting life and death struggles on the *Mayflower* voyage across the Atlantic and survives the bitter first winter in the New World.
ISBN 9781645169840
[1. Historical Fiction]

Published and Distributed by MVP Kids Media, LLC - Mesa, Arizona, USA
Printed by Prosperous Printing Inc. - Shenzhen, China

MVP Kids First Edition: March 2020
www.mvpkids.com
Written by Carol Sauder
Illustration and design by Stephanie Strouse

WELCOME to the WORLD OF

mvpkids®

Entertainment with PURPOSE®

Everything we create is with the intention of nurturing a child's character. Our mission is to equip parents, teachers, and caregivers to engage with kids through inspiring entertainment.

nurture LITERACY™

cultivate MENTORSHIP™

inspire CHARACTER®

expand EDUCATION™

enrich ENTERTAINMENT™

BLAKE AND THE MYSTERIOUS COIN™ SERIES

Book One - *To the New World and Back*™

mvpkids

DNA CHRONICLES™

SOPHIA DAY®

DEAR READER,

Your DNA is unique! Miraculously copied into each of your cells, your genetic code, using just four nucleotides, determines your eye and hair color, the complexion of your skin, your height, your nose, your ears, and much, much more about how you look. Did you know that the strands of DNA molecules within your body stretched end to end would reach to the moon and back more than 61 times? Your unique DNA code is a patchwork of the many generations in your lineage since the beginning of time.

But there is so much more to who you are than science can define by your genetic code. The personal experiences and life stories of your ancestors have molded your "historical DNA™," an element of who you are as a person. The fusion of your unique scientific DNA with your just-as-unique "historical DNA™" forms a collage unlike any other in existence.

My DNA Chronicles™ series seeks to explore the life experiences of the ancestors of our MVP Kids. Some of the adventures are fictional, but the historical characters and events reflect actual accounts of those who lived it. I have not glossed over the challenges nor modernized the norms and sensitivities to suit today's times. It is my intention to inspire you to experience history by considering the unique personalities, thoughts, feelings, and actions of those who participated in it. I challenge you to learn about your own "historical DNA™" and the rich and complex experiences of your ancestors. And remember to enjoy your daily journey. Every day you write a new page in your very own history book.

Sophia Day

Contents

Blake and the Mysterious Coin™

BOOK ONE

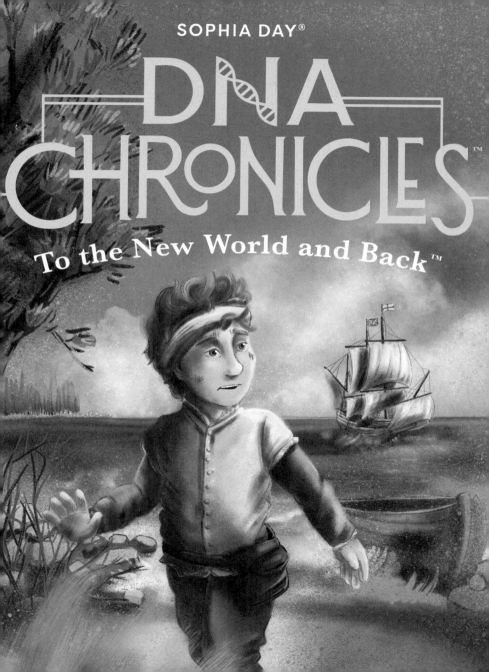

Walking, I am listening to a deeper way.

Suddenly all my ancestors are behind me.

Be still, they say. Watch and listen. You

are the result of the love of thousands.

Linda Hogan (b. 1947)

NATIVE AMERICAN WRITER

CHAPTER ONE
TURKEY BLUES

Blake sat at his computer, lost in the excitement of trying to win his superheroes video game and advance to the next level. He had been here so many times before, always ready to slay the alien and fight hand in hand with his mighty hero, Gaelic, overpower his enemies, and move to the next galaxy, but—*BAM!!!!* Lightning started flashing. The entire world exploded in one mega blast, and he was thrown into space. Searching through the debris, he found his laser and returned to earth defeated....again. He was very annoyed and frustrated that he couldn't get beyond this level. His friends were at least a level ahead of him and teased him about it at school. *Augh...what is my problem?*

Once he started, it was always so hard to stop playing this game. He knew he should be doing his history homework and studying, but he just couldn't get motivated. History is so boring, and who really cares what happened in the past? He was trying to convince himself that it was okay, but he knew he would be in trouble if he didn't start on his homework when he came home from school. That was a major rule in the James' house! Homework first, and then chores.

Suddenly the kitchen door slammed shut, and his mother came in carrying grocery bags.

"Hi, Blake! How was your day? Can you help me carry the groceries in from the car? I had to stop at the store on the way home, and I had an exhausting day at work. I finally finished the design project I've been working on for months."

Blake jumped up from the sofa and headed to the garage.

"Okay, Mom."

He started to mumble to himself as he gathered up the groceries. "I am tired, too! And I had a crazy day at school! It may not be rocket science, but eighth grade is hard. All the homework and trying to keep up my grades. Where is Jackson or Layla or Annie? Why can't they help?"

After he carried in the last grocery bag, he headed back to the sofa.

"Blake, will you please help me put these groceries away?" Mom asked. "I'm running late and need to start dinner. Your dad is working late, and Jackson had to stay late for football practice."

Well, I guess nobody really cares about the kind of day I had! Blake moaned. He was feeling a little sorry for himself.

After he put the groceries in the pantry and the last gallon of milk in the fridge, he started to head back to the family room, but his mom called out to him again. "Blake, I know you have homework, but I think you'd better go feed the horses first. If they don't have their feed by 6:30, they will be out there complaining and racing around the arena." Mom reached in the snack jar and tossed him his favorite energy bar. She winked and smiled at him because usually snacks weren't allowed right before dinner.

"Thanks, Mom!" Blake said.

What next? He headed out to the barn. None of his friends lived on a ranch or had to do chores. His mood was not getting better. As he stepped into the barn chewing his last bite of the energy bar, he could smell the sweet scent of the hay and hear the persistent nickers of the horses. They were hungry, pacing around and trying to chase each other away from the fence.

He had to admit, he did love the horses and the way they had their own personalities, just like people. You had to watch out for Ben. He was feisty and thought he owned the whole arena and the pastures, too. Everyone called him "Biting Ben" because he would nip at you, especially if you weren't paying attention to him. And he always expected to eat first.

Blake sat down on the bench and changed into his mucking boots. His favorite mare was Rosie. She was the color of a shiny new copper penny, especially after he brushed her. She would always come trotting to him with her head held high like she was showing off just for him. He started to feel his anxiety and bad mood melt away as he spread the hay around the arena into separate flakes for the five horses. Rosie kept bumping him from behind. She wanted him to play.

"Sorry, girl, I've got lots to do tonight. Wait until Saturday, and I promise we'll go for a ride!"

She went trotting over to her feed and started eating. She didn't want to share her dinner with the other horses. *Rosie is like me; she loves her food!*

He heard his brother Jackson's car as he drove up the driveway. Jackson saw him in the arena and headed down to talk to him.

"Hey, how was practice?" Blake greeted him. "Do you think you'll get to start on Friday?"

Jackson looked hot and exhausted but had a big smile on his face. "Coach said he's planning on me starting at linebacker. It's going to be a great game."

They headed up to the house together when Blake unexpectedly tackled Jackson and started to wrestle with him on the ground. He loved to hang out with his brother, even though Jackson was four years older. Blake was strong for his age and loved to challenge his older brother to wrestling matches.

"Blake, stop! I'm tired and I don't want to get hurt before this game."

"I'm sorry, I just wasn't thinking about that!" said Blake.

Jackson reached down, grabbed his brother's hand, and lifted him to his feet. He ruffled his hair and put his arm around him as they headed to the house again. A brotherly truce had been called. When they reached the house, Jackson headed upstairs to clean up for dinner.

Outside, they could hear Dad's pickup truck in the driveway, and then the girls talking and laughing as they headed into the house.

"Dad and the girls are home!" Blake shouted into the kitchen. He always loved all the activity when everyone was home.

"Hi, Blake." Dad grinned as the screen door slammed behind him. You could see he had worked hard that day. His tee shirt was covered with dirt and sweat, and his hair looked like it had a mind of its own, but he was still smiling and teasing everyone. He left his muddy boots at the back door, rushed over to give their mom a great big hug and kiss, and did a couple dance steps with her around the kitchen island. *It is never boring with him around.*

Once, when Blake was working hard with his dad digging fence post holes, he asked him, "How do you stay so happy even when you've had a hard day? Don't you feel like just sitting down and complaining about how tired you are?" It had been a very hot day, Blake's arms were sore from digging in the hard dirt, and the flies and insects kept buzzing around his sweaty face. It was very annoying.

"Of course, I do. Everyone does sometimes. But life is too short to waste it feeling sorry for myself. My attitude affects me and everyone around me, so I choose to stay positive. Do you want me to be grumpy and negative?"

"No! I like you just the way you are!"

"Blake, you just have to keep working at it."

I don't think I can ever do that, Blake thought.

"What happens if you fail?"

"Blake, we all fail sometimes. That's how we learn. No one is perfect. Remember when you saddled Rosie up the first time by yourself? What happened?"

"The saddle wasn't tight enough, and I fell off, saddle and all! It was embarrassing. It scared Rosie, and she took off galloping across the arena!"

"What did you do next?"

"I figured out that I didn't cinch the saddle strap tight enough, so I double-checked everything to make sure it was right. Then I had to convince Rosie it was okay to let me try again. She was spooked. When I saddled her the second time, I stayed on and the saddle stayed on. Rosie wasn't sure she trusted me."

"Did you get better?"

"It took practice, but now I saddle her, and I don't even think about what I'm doing. It just comes naturally. And Rosie really trusts me now."

"You just had to keep working at it until you got it right!"

"You're right, Dad. Guess you can't give up. That's when you really fail."

After dinner, Dad was getting ready to go out the door with Jackson to finish the evening chores when he turned to Blake and said casually, "I hear you had a little trouble in your history class today."

Blake's history teacher, Mr. Wilson, was a friend of his father's. They had been roommates in college.

"He said you don't take the class seriously, and you're always clowning around." Dad continued, a disappointed look on his face. "We'll talk about it when I finish my evening chores."

Oh, no! I didn't think Mr. Wilson would call my dad. Blake went to his room and started working on his homework. He could feel his stomach start to do flips. They had had several talks before about being respectful to his teachers at school. He knew his dad would take it very seriously.

Blake had to admit that Mr. Wilson was a good teacher. He always tried to make the class interesting, but Blake just couldn't get into history. Today the class had been studying about the *Mayflower*, Pilgrims, and the first Thanksgiving. Mr. Wilson had been really excited about the lesson, his eyes lighting up as he told the class, "I want history to come alive for you, just as if you are standing alongside our nation's early European settlers! All of the freedoms we take for granted started in an unknown wilderness on November 9, 1620. The Pilgrims courageously chose to cross the Atlantic in a quest for religious freedom. Without their courage, where would we be today? There's an interesting true story about a young indentured servant on the *Mayflower* named John Howland. Because the route to America was expensive, indentured servants typically worked four to seven years in exchange for their passage. Well, John Howland fell overboard in a violent storm, but was rescued when they hauled him back on board. If he had not been saved that day, there would be no Presidents Theodore Roosevelt, George Bush, or George W. Bush, because they are all direct descendants of John Howland.

"Can you see how the past, our history, has set the path for our future? Your future! You are writing your own history book. Okay, that's a great note to end on for today. I need to go to the office to copy the study guide for tomorrow. While I'm gone, take this time to study."

As soon as the door shut, Blake tried to study, but he was getting antsy—American History was the last class of the day. *I am SOOO ready to be gone!* He started thinking about his video game and how he could advance to the next level. As he was daydreaming and staring out one of the windows Mr. Wilson had left open, he noticed a few beetles climbing up and down the pane. It was fall, and many of the bugs were anxious to find homes before winter set in.

Suddenly, Hannah, who sat right behind him, let out a blood-curdling scream. Blake had never had someone behind him scream in his ear like that—he jumped up so fast that he nearly tipped his desk over, turning around quickly to see what was wrong. There was the culprit, a huge black beetle with pincers that were opening and closing. It must have taken advantage of the open window to crawl inside. Hannah was sitting on the top of her desk with her feet on the seat.

Here is my chance…Blake to the rescue!

They had these beetles on the ranch and their turkeys loved to chase them around and eat them. Blake jumped up, grabbed the beetle between his thumb and forefinger, and started acting like he was a turkey. A Thanksgiving turkey, right?

Because they had two turkeys at home, he was very good at mimicking them. He started strutting around and pecking at his classmates and dangling the squirming beetle in their faces. The girls all screamed whenever he got close to them with the squirming bug. He was funny and everyone was laughing, except for Sarah in the third row. She always told him he needed to grow up, but he still liked to show off in front of her.

I bet I could get an Academy Award for this performance. "And this year's winner is Blake James!" The crowd roared in approval. Blake's imagination was working overtime.

The door opened, and Blake was caught in the middle of the room prancing around gobbling, with the squirming bug in hand. When he looked up and saw Mr. Wilson standing in the doorway, he tripped over a desk leg and fell into the map, which crashed to the floor. Sheepishly, he stood and returned to his desk.

"Mr. Blake James! It seems you must be looking for something extra to occupy all your spare time," Mr. Wilson said, walking over to his desk and placing the study guides on its edge. "Because you were supposed to be studying, that wonderful performance entitles you to write a special report about life as a Pilgrim. Maybe your amazing knowledge of turkeys will come in handy. I think you need to consider where and when you do your turkey impressions in the future."

The dismissal bell rang.

"Everyone please take a copy of tomorrow's study guide from my desk. Blake, please stay, fix the map, and deposit your monster beetle back where he or she came from."

He wanted to explain to Mr. Wilson about the open window, the scream, and the bug, and that he didn't mean to get carried away, but he just stood there and turned red.

All thoughts of an Academy Award went back out the window with the squirming beetle.

CHAPTER TWO

A STEP IN TIME

He kept trying to concentrate on studying and finishing his homework, but all he could see was the disappointed look on his dad's face. *I don't think my dad will appreciate my performance, either.*

Blake really loved his dad and hated to think he had let him down. There was a tapping at the door.

"Come in."

His dad entered the room. Blake was relieved to finally get this talk over with.

"Tell me what happened, Blake."

Blake started to tell him the story and felt very sheepish. When he finished, his dad sat down beside him.

"What do you think the consequences of your turkey behavior should be?"

"Well, sir, I have to write a special report about Pilgrims. I think that should be enough. I'm really sorry I did it."

Blake's dad was silent for a while.

"Blake, I want you to go to Mr. Wilson tomorrow and apologize for your behavior. This affected your whole class. And I expect more of you, too. You need to think before you act. It will save you a lot of trouble in your life. We are all responsible for our own actions."

They both sat there silently for a while. He could tell his father was trying to come up with something that would teach him a lesson.

Finally, Dad started to speak. "I'm sure you remember when my father came and asked us if we could store all the old furniture and things from my great-great-grandmother? Her name was Clara James, and she was the family historian. Let me tell you, she saved a lot of stuff, and it's all up in the loft of the barn."

Blake laughed. "Dad, I remember when it all came a couple months ago on the truck from Pennsylvania. Do you know how many trips we made up and down those stairs? I don't think she threw anything away!"

They both laughed, and Blake felt some of his tension fade. It felt good to laugh with his dad again.

"Well, Blake, I think we have a lot of heirlooms to sort through! And I think I'm going to put you in charge of organizing and sorting it out. Maybe you will learn to appreciate history by searching through some of our own history. Let's meet up in the hayloft on Saturday and see just what needs to be done. You may find something that you can use in your report for Mr. Wilson." He patted Blake on the back and went out the door.

I guess it could be worse, thought Blake. He wasn't crazy about the idea of spending Saturday morning looking through junk in the barn loft, but he knew better than to complain. *Maybe if I give it my best shot on Saturday, Dad will show some mercy and only make me do it one day.*

The next day in Mr. Wilson's class, Blake waited until everyone left the room after the bell rang.

"Mr. Wilson, I want to apologize for my behavior yesterday. I really am sorry."

"Well, Blake, thank you for coming to me," Mr. Wilson said. "I'm hoping your research paper will help you find a connection to history. It will be due in two weeks and I'm looking forward to reading it."

Blake nodded. He was glad he talked to Mr. Wilson, but he had no idea what he would write about!

Saturday morning dawned, and Blake turned over and pulled the blanket over his head just as the sun started streaming through the sides of the blinds. He wished he could just lie there and have a lazy morning, but he knew his dad would be expecting him early in the barn loft. He rolled out of bed and grabbed his jeans beside the bed. He would be needing his work clothes today. He washed his face with cold water, grabbed his baseball cap to hide his wild hair, and headed downstairs for breakfast.

"Morning, Blake," his mom greeted him. "I hear you have an *appointment* in the hayloft. I'm excited to see what you find! I've wanted to go up there and look for treasures, but I just haven't had the time."

Blake's mom always loved going to antique stores and yard sales and looking for fun things to use in her decorating business. They had spent many days at auctions and flea markets.

"Maybe later you can do your turkey impressions for me," she teased gently.

Blake's face turned red; he was embarrassed. Dad must have told her the whole story.

He finished his breakfast. Time to get started. He headed out the door into the fall morning. The air was cool, crisp, and had started to smell like fall. You could hear the insects and cicadas singing their noisy end-of-summer songs. His boots crunched in the gravel, seeming to keep a cadence with the many sounds. He hoped this project wasn't going to be as painful as he expected. *Spending this beautiful morning looking at old junk and piles of old smelly boxes isn't my idea of a good time.*

Off in the distance, he could see dark clouds starting to fill the sky. *I hope it doesn't storm. I promised Rosie that I would saddle her up for a ride today.*

Dad and Jackson were already in the barn feeding the horses and all their other farm animals. He could hear them talking as they went about their work. Dad was always going to auctions and bringing home new animals. They had five horses, a bull, six cows, some goats, chickens, lambs, dogs, cats, and of course, two turkeys!

I will never forget those turkeys! Blake's mind flashed back to history class. *How in the world will I get that report written in time? And what am I going to write about? I wish I had never decided to show off in class.*

He waved at Dad and Jackson, but they were too busy with their work to notice him as he headed inside the barn. He took the steps two at a time up to the top. "Wow, what a mess!" He had forgotten just how many "heirlooms" were stored in this section of the loft.

Everyone always said Blake had a knack for organizing and solving problems, but this was overwhelming. *Oh well, one step at a time, right? Maybe I'll only have to do it today.* He sat down on a little stool that he pulled off the top of a stack of boxes. It was a cool looking stool that had three peg legs.

"I bet this was a milking stool!" He didn't realize he said it out loud.

"What did you say?" He hadn't heard his dad come up the stairs.

"Look at this, Dad! An old milking stool—it's so cool! I bet this was used on the family farm that was in Pennsylvania. Mom is going to love this!"

His dad picked it up and examined it.

"It is definitely handmade. Look at the axe marks on the peg legs. And you're right, it's a milking stool. I saw one at an auction. The early pioneers had to make everything by hand. It was the only way they could get their furniture, tools, and other items for the farm— they couldn't run to the store like we do. Your Grandpa James said he thought our ancestors Peter and Clara lived in a log cabin. He visited the farm when he was a young boy before his family moved out west. Maybe we can ask him about it the next time he comes to visit."

Blake was trying to resist the idea that he might like doing this project. "Maybe I'll find even more things that we can ask him about!"

They both stood there looking around the room. The dust particles were swirling around in the sunlight streaming through the barn window. There was a feeling in the room that was hard to explain. It was like contentment and anticipation for something still unfound. It just felt good. They heard thunder off in the distance, and Dad glanced at the window.

"Sounds like a storm might be brewing. I've got to get back to the chores, but I'll check on you in a couple hours. I can help you move the heavy boxes and furniture when I get back. Any questions?"

"No, sir."

Blake heard his father's footsteps on the creaky wooden stairs as he headed back through the barn and outside again.

He started looking around the room. Wow! He had no idea what was in the boxes and old trunks, or what he was going to do with the stuff that was inside. *This is going to take forever!*

He walked around trying to decide what to do first. He bumped into a cardboard box, which fell apart and spilled papers on the floor. His eyes went to the back of the room. There was an old desk that was hidden behind a tall dresser. *Maybe I can use the desk to help organize these papers and interesting things I might find.*

It was a good thing Blake was strong. He was able to push the dresser out of the way to get to the desk. Everything had a thick layer of dust. He took his shirt sleeve and wiped off the top of the desk, sneezing as the tiny dust particles filled the air.

The oak desk was a warm honey color. He started opening little drawers and looking inside. On the back was etched a name and date: *Peter James to Clara, my loving wife, March* 1820.

Could this desk really be almost 200 years old? And the last name is James! It was a very simple desk, but it was so well made. The drawer and drawer fronts were notched and fit perfectly together. You could see it had been made by hand. The drawer on the left was stuck, and when he tugged on it, it came out completely. When he tried to put it back, it just wouldn't fit.

Oh, no! I hope I didn't break it!

Blake sat down on the little milking stool and started to examine the drawer. At the very back, a small piece of splintered wood was sticking up.

When he touched it, the back of the drawer came off.

What is this? It looks like a secret hiding place. The back of the drawer had been a false one, to fool someone. *What could this be?* When he picked up the false back of the drawer, he saw a small piece of folded paper. It was so old and brittle that when he touched it, a piece of the corner cracked and fell to the ground. *This is so fragile.* Slowly and carefully, he unfolded it and spread it out on the desktop.

According to family history, this coin was given to our ancestor Henry Samson on December 25, 1620 on the Mayflower. It has been treasured as a family heirloom and passed down to the firstborn child of each generation since that date. Please keep it safe. Signed: Peter James, 1850.

Coin? What coin? Blake had not seen a coin.

He carefully refolded the crumbling paper and put it back in the drawer before taking a closer look inside for the coin. *There it is—just inside the front, wedged in a small crack!* It was tarnished and looked like silver, but he couldn't read the inscription very well. As he grabbed the coin, a bolt of lightning lit up the room, accompanied by a deafening peal of thunder that shook the whole barn. The room started to spin around and around, faster and faster. He didn't have time to think about anything except the pain in his ears. The last thing he saw was the dust spiraling in the air as his knees hit the wooden floor.

Everything went blank.

CHAPTER THREE
THE AWAKENING

"Where am I? It's so dark!" Blake saw Jackson ahead and frantically called out to him.

"Jackson, wait for me! Where are we going?" Jackson ignored him. "Wait for me! Where are we? Please answer me." Blake followed him up a strange ladder and outside into a howling wind. The rain was coming down in torrents. Without warning, Jackson was gone—a freezing wave of water had grabbed him and sent him flying into a black hole. Blake stood and pushed against the wind as hard as he could.

"Help! Help, my brother just disappeared into the storm. Please, help me find him! You have to find him!" Blake could barely hear his own voice as he scrambled to stand on the slippery surface. Men came running as Blake pulled himself up to a rail and peered into the darkness.

"There, that's where he disappeared! You have to save him!"

The icy water hit Blake and slammed him down. As his body hurled forward, his head hit something hard, knocking him out.

Everything went blank again.

Blake awoke to the sound of his own moaning. His head ached so badly he thought it would split open.

He leaned over and threw up all over the floor.

What kind of a dream is this? Or...I guess nightmare is more like it. He lay back down, but his body continued to sway gently back and forth.

Where am I? What is happening to me? The last thing he remembered was being in the barn, upstairs in the hayloft. He knew his dad and Jackson had been outside doing the Saturday morning chores. He remembered a bright flash of lightning and a loud clap of thunder, and then he had been trying to find Jackson. *This doesn't make any sense! Nothing makes any sense!*

"Dad! Dad help me! Jackson, please! Did you find Jackson? Can anyone hear me? Help me, I don't know what's happening to me!"

He could hear the strange sounds of activity in the space he was in. He didn't know what the smells were around him, but they sickened him again. He leaned over and threw up a second time. Someone touched his cheek and placed a cool cloth on his forehead.

"Mom, is that you? I feel so sick! What's happening to me? Did you find Jackson?" He felt the cloth being removed and heard it being rinsed clean before it was placed back on his head. The coolness felt good on his throbbing head.

He felt the closeness as someone leaned in and placed a cup to his lips.

"Drink this, Henry, and you will feel better. The storm is starting to fade and the winds on the sea are dying down. Just rest. I promise I won't leave you until you are better. Just rest now. You're going to get better."

Blake tried to open his eyes, but nothing made sense to him. It was dark and he could hear a child crying somewhere, and people talking and whispering around him.

"Mom? Mom, is that you?" He closed his eyes and sank deeper into a swirling darkness that carried him away again.

A dream, this has to be a dream!

Who is Henry?

He could not tell how long he had been sleeping, but he felt his stomach reminding him it had been a long time since he ate breakfast. How long ago was that? None of the sounds or smells were familiar. *Where am I?* He slowly opened his eyes a little and tried to sit up, but weakness overcame him.

"Henry, don't try to get up. You are too weak, and I don't want you to fall and hit your head again."

He opened his eyes fully and stared into the face of a woman who was a complete stranger! *Why is she calling me Henry, and why am I here?* Fear grabbed him again and he started to panic. He wanted to get out of there fast, but she held him down when he tried to move away.

"Henry, try not to exert yourself. You've been sickened by the sea and the waves pounding our ship. You fell when you were on the deck, trying to help rescue your friend John Howland. Do you remember? He fell overboard in the fierce storm, but you were able to help the crew find him. It pleased God to save his life and yours. Why did you and John leave the hull and go above the gratings in such a storm? You hit your head when a wave caught you and threw you against the planks. And John is still weakened from his misadventure, but the doctor says he will live."

John Howland? That name sounds familiar. Where have I heard it before? He lay there quietly trying to gather his thoughts. He heard the voice of his American History teacher, Mr. Wilson "I want history to come alive for you, just as if you are standing alongside our nation's early European settlers!" *I remember he told us about John Howland falling off the Mayflower in a storm and then being rescued! I remember it was John Howland. JOHN HOWLAND!*

NO WAY! Don't panic, Blake. Don't panic, don't panic! This can't be happening! He tried to keep his eyes closed and will himself back to sleep. *Maybe I can wake up and be back home working in the hayloft, sorting through the ancient stuff. And I promised Rosie that I would ride her today. The COIN! It must have something to do with the coin.* He remembered finding it hidden in the secret compartment of the desk, examining it, and then suddenly the lightning hit.

And now I am in this strange dream.

"I want history to come alive for you...I want history to come alive for you...I want...history...history...history........." Mr. Wilson's prophetic words echoed over and over in his throbbing head until sleep finally captured him.

———

When he opened his eyes again, he could see the woman resting on the floor with her head leaning against his cot. He silently studied her for a moment. Her eyes were closed, and she looked tired. It was cramped and dim where she sat. A wooden bucket filled with water sat on the floor behind her. On the rim, he saw the cloth she had used to wipe his brow and cool his aching head.

She must have been here the whole time, caring for me and calming my fears. She called me Henry. Am I really on the Mayflower? He tried to think through his current circumstances. *I have no idea how this is going to end, but I know I have to see it through. Well, here goes...*

"Mother... is that you?" Blake quietly whispered the words.

The woman stirred and sat up. The weariness left her eyes as she touched his cheek and tears of joy streamed down her face.

"Oh, Henry, you are back! I have been so worried that you would not recover." She sat there and sobbed as she hugged him. "I thank God that He has returned you to me!"

She grabbed the cloth that rested on the bucket, dipped it in the water, and wiped his forehead. She dipped it again and wiped away her tears.

"I am here, but I don't remember much." *Maybe I can use the excuse of the head injury to gather information.* "You told me about my friend John Howland falling overboard, but I don't remember anything that happened before that, Mother."

"Henry, don't you know who I am? I am your Aunt Ann Tilley. You came with your Uncle Edward and me and your baby cousin, Humility, to help us in America. You fell and hit your head during the storm seven days ago, and I have been here taking care of you. The doctor was worried you wouldn't wake up. We all are very weakened by the perils and sickness aboard, but you have survived."

She called softly to a young girl who was sitting nearby on a mat of some sort.

"Lizzy, go and fetch the doctor! Hurry! Tell him that Henry is awake!"

Lizzy stood and peered at Blake before leaving. She seemed to be about the age of his sister Annie. He felt a wave of homesickness hit him. *Where is my family? Will I ever see them again?*

"Aunt Ann, I thought I heard a baby crying in my dreams. Was that Humility? Is she here now?"

"She has been staying with the Brewsters. When you were injured, I had to care for you day and night. Mary Brewster would bring her over to see us whenever she could slip away from her own family. We were praying that you would hear Humility and it would help you wake up. You probably heard her crying when it was time to go. She never wanted to leave. She really misses us, and she will be so happy to see you." Aunt Ann's eyes teared up again. "It will be wonderful to have you both back again."

Lizzy returned in a few minutes with a man about his father's age.

"Dr. Fuller, Henry is awake!" Aunt Ann exclaimed. "But he says he cannot remember anything that happened before he fell and hit his head."

The doctor sat down and examined Blake. He looked tired and weary, but he was very caring and careful as he looked Blake over. Finally, he smiled and said, "Henry, I see no reason you should not recover. It may take time for your memory to return, but you seem to be in good health considering your ordeal. Maybe you and John can explain why you went above the gratings during such a fierce storm. You certainly were not using good judgment and are very blessed to have been saved from such a terrible death at the mercy of the sea! I pray this experience will teach you both to think before you act in the future. We are headed to a new life in the wilderness and you need to stop your folly. There will be hard labor as we build new homes and grow accustomed to living in a new world that we know nothing of. You will need to be up to the task, young Henry Samson.

Don't squander your health for no good reason!"

Blake was a little embarrassed by Henry's behavior, even though he wasn't Henry.

"Thank you, Doctor. I am sorry." *Wow! I can't believe that I really felt the impact of Henry's and John's actions. Maybe pretending to be this Henry character won't be too hard. We seem to have some things in common!*

The doctor left with a final pat on Blake's shoulder.

Aunt Ann soon left as well and then returned with food and something to drink. It all looked and smelled very strange. There was a biscuit that was dry and very crumbly, which reminded him of the time Mom found an old biscuit under the cabinet in the pantry— it was so dry and old even the dog wouldn't eat it. Aunt Ann had also brought a little butter for the biscuit, some peas, and meat that looked like the beef jerky he would buy from their neighbor, old Mr. Frank, at the fair. It wasn't what he was used to, but Blake was so hungry that he would have eaten anything. The drink in the tin cup smelled like vinegar and stinky socks, but he drank it right down anyway.

"Be careful not to eat too fast, Henry. Your stomach may not be able to handle all this food. And we don't want to waste any of our food, for we started late on this journey and our supplies are getting low."

"Thank you, Aunt Ann. I'll be careful."

CHAPTER FOUR
A NEW "OLD" FRIEND

When Blake finished eating, he sat up and looked around. He felt a little better. He still had a headache, but it wasn't throbbing anymore. It was dark and there were people huddled around on floor mats. He could see blankets hanging on ropes to give privacy to some areas. Someone was reading stories, and he heard children laughing and singing. It was comforting to hear the children. The ship was still rocking and causing anything that wasn't securely fastened to move; even his mat moved back and forth a little bit within the area that they lived. He suddenly felt waves of seasickness as well as homesickness rock his body.

Blake could hear the loud voices of men talking and laughing as well. There really was no such thing as privacy here. He thought of the bedroom that he shared with his brother Jackson. *Does anyone even know I'm gone?* Tears stung his eyes.

"Hey, John Howland, I hear you were trying to swim back to

London!"

Blake had no idea who was talking or where the voices were coming from. Everyone in the area started to laugh, but the sound was interrupted by bouts of wheezing and coughing. Curious, Blake decided to get up and see what the commotion was about. He was weak and dizzy, but he headed in the direction of the laughter only to find someone sitting in the middle of a group of men.

"John Howland, it was the Lord himself who put that rope in your hand!" one of the men said. "Tell us, son, your account of the accident that should have sent you into the deep angry sea and to the meeting of your Maker!"

"Ah, yes, I agree with you Elder Brewster," said the young man in the middle of the older men. "I am here but by the grace of God! Henry Samson and I were seeking some relief from the stench between the decks. We were told not to go up to the deck, but thought it would bring us no harm. As soon as I lifted the hatch, a huge wave sent me reeling over the side of the ship. I went down into the icy darkness. The cold started to numb me, and I just wanted to close my eyes and sleep forever.

"But then, I heard my mother's voice calling to me, 'John, wake up! Wake up, John! You're sailing to the New World. You must not give up. Wake up!' I could see her face as she and my brothers stood at the pier in London and waved good-bye as we sailed off in the *Mayflower*.

"My eyes were burning from the saltwater and my lungs felt like they would explode. Suddenly, I saw the *Mayflower* above me, and I grabbed a rope dancing in front of me. The water was freezing, and I felt myself being rescued from the sea. That is all I remember until I woke up in the cabin with Mistress Carver nursing me back to life. And now I am on my way to find Henry and hear his tale. I heard he has been taken ill, but is recovering."

John looked up and saw Henry. "Oh, what a sight you are for sore eyes, my friend!" He headed to Blake and gave him the biggest bear hug he ever had in his life. Blake was overwhelmed by John's story and wasn't sure how he should greet this friend that he had never met before, except in history class.

"Henry, I heard from Lizzy Tilley that you hit your head on the deck trying to save me. I thank you, my friend, with all my heart. We were very foolish to try to go above the grate! But let me thank you again and praise our Creator that we both were saved!" John could not speak without tears streaming down his face, and continued to give Blake several hugs as he spoke.

Blake could barely breathe each time John gave him a hug. "John, you don't need to thank me that much or I won't survive! It will be me who's thrown overboard to a watery grave!" They both laughed. It felt good to laugh and share the moment with this new, yet old, friend.

"You know, John, I have no recollection of anything before the storm. The doctor said my memory might return, but I will have to rely on you to help me understand what has happened. I will try to not be a burden to you. When I awoke, I did not even recognize my Aunt Ann! And even being on this ship is all new to me. I feel like a stranger here from another place."

I really am a stranger from another place—and another time! Everything is strange to me. I cannot tell John the real story. Not yet, anyway. And how could I tell John Howland that I just read about him in my history book? It is just too unbelievable!

"Come with me to the deck. The sea is calmer today and we can try not to get into trouble again. I think the fresh air would do us both good."

Blake nodded in agreement as they said goodbye to the men, and he followed John to the ladder that led to the deck. He remembered climbing it the night he thought he was following his brother Jackson. As they climbed, both had to keep their heads low so they wouldn't hit the rafters.

John lifted the grate and they both climbed onto the deck. Blake was amazed and speechless as he looked about the *Mayflower*. It was not as big as he had imagined it to be when he read about it. The sky was so blue above them and the breeze was light and steady—a vast difference to the night of the storm. John led him over to the side of the ship.

"This is where I fell off the ship, Henry. This is where you sent the men to find me!" They both stared into the ocean below as they watched the swell of the ocean lift the boat up and down in a steady forward motion. *I am so thankful I did not fall into the sea!* The sails were open fully to the wind as the crew continued to do their jobs. He looked up and counted three masts, five sails, and saw a massive amount of rope rigging. At the front of the ship, a sailor kept a lookout from behind a large square-looking sail that was attached to a smaller mast pointing forward. In a corner of the deck, he saw another sailor busy sewing a sail. Blake started to feel his stomach and head rebel against the constant moving of the ship. John looked over and saw he was turning green.

"Henry, take a deep breath and don't look down. Keep your eyes on the horizon and face forward until you feel right again."

Blake listened to his friend and gradually started to feel better. They both stood on the deck for a while until one of the crew started mocking them for being seasick and chased them away.

"Go back down to the women and children where you belong. We have work to do!"

"Sorry, sir, we did not mean to interrupt your work." John waved and smiled at the man, and then walked with Blake to the opposite side of the ship.

"Henry, for the most part, we can come to the deck when the weather is good. We try not to get in the way of the captain and crew, for they have their jobs to do. In the beginning of our journey, there was a sailor who was very profane and tormented us day after day. He would mock us for being people of faith and curse at us, declaring that he hoped to see us die and cast overboard. We wanted to just get along with everyone, but he harassed us all the time, no matter how kind we tried to be to him. When we were halfway on this journey, he was struck down by a grievous disease, and it was his body that was thrown overboard."

Blake certainly had run into his share of bullies at school. His dad told him that when someone puts another person down or bullies others, it gives them a sense of power they are lacking. *I never thought of bullies being on the Mayflower.*

They both returned to the grate and headed down to the hull where they lived. When they got to the bottom, they had to stoop again. It felt very confined.

"Henry, I need to get back to Master Carver, for I have errands to run and I want to see if they have need of me. I've tried to be a good servant to the Carvers, and they have treated me very well. I have almost four years of service owed to them and then I'll be on my own. I'll see you tomorrow and trust we are both greatly improved in our health." He raised his hand in a wave as he made his way back to the Carvers.

Blake felt a wave of homesickness hit him as his new friend hurried away. *Does anyone miss me at home?* He could picture his mom and sisters working in the garden and Rosie showing off in the arena. *Well, one thing's for sure, I'm not home right now.*

Blake started to study his new surroundings as best he could in the dim light. It seemed there were many people in their beds, and he heard coughing and murmuring.

"Master Henry, it's good to see you up and around. We were all worried about you, but you were getting very good care from your Aunt Ann. She didn't leave your side. Make sure you thank her, lad." It was one of men that had been talking to him and John. He could barely sit up, and his teeth were all rancid and black. "Son, I hope we get to America soon because we are getting sicker, and our supplies are running low."

"I'm very sorry that you don't feel well. Can I get you something to drink?" Blake felt so bad seeing all the sickness and suffering.

"Thanks, Henry. If you could get my cup and ladle some aqua vitae into it, I would greatly appreciate it." Blake wanted to help him, even though he had no idea what "aqua vitae" was.

"Sir, did you know I have no memory of anything prior to my injury? I'm sorry, but I don't remember your name. And what is 'aqua vitae'?" Blake felt a little guilty pretending to lose his memory, but how else would he explain his ignorance at his surroundings and life here?

The man started to laugh, and then it turned into a wheezy cough. "My name is James Chilton. Pleased to meet you again, Henry Samson. I came on board the *Mayflower* with my wife and my daughter, Mary. You will probably see Mary around helping to care for the children. She is 13 years old. I am 64 years old and the oldest passenger on board. And since you don't remember what we have been drinking the whole voyage, I will try to enlighten you. Since there is no safe drinking water available, we all drink beer and aqua vitae, which is made of distilled wine or brandy. It's the only safe thing to drink on the ship."

"Thank you, sir. I remember drinking something when I first awakened that had a sour vinegar smell, and I had no idea what it was. And sir, could you tell me how long we have been on our journey, and when you expect we'll reach America?"

"Well, we have been here longer than expected. We have been at sea about two months. Many delays and the storms have slowed us down. I expect we are a few weeks away from our destination."

Mr. Chilton handed Blake his cup and pointed to the container that held the drink. Inside was a ladle. Blake filled his cup and handed it back to him.

"Thank you, Master Samson. I was thirsty, and this should help my cough."

"I hope you will start to feel better soon. I need to go now and see if my Aunt Ann needs me. It was a pleasure to meet you…again!"

Blake smiled and waved goodbye to Mr. Chilton as he went to find Aunt Ann.

CHAPTER FIVE
PERILOUS JOURNEY

B lake spent the next couple of days helping with chores and following John Howland around. Everything was so different, and it fascinated him. One day they went to the very bottom of the ship, which was called the "hold," to get more candles. There Blake saw bushels of oatmeal, mustard seed, and peas; barrels of beer and aqua vitae; and stores of dried beef, dried fish, salt pork, vinegar, butter, soap, water, biscuits, cheese, gallons of sweet oil, candles, and firewood. And the smell of the dried fish was overpowering. Blake could see that supplies were dwindling.

As they moved about in the tight quarters, they entered an area filled with a variety of items. "Here are many kinds of equipment we will need in the New World, and there was one piece we had to use on this ship. It was an iron screw stored in this area. It saved the *Mayflower* and our lives." John said. "Henry, do you remember any of this?"

"No, John, but I would like to hear all about it. It might help me remember something."

"Well, it was just weeks after leaving England and we were caught in a really vicious storm. Everyone was holding tight to a rope or bulkhead for dear life. Some of the women and children were even tied to the post to be kept from being swept away.

"Suddenly, there was a wrenching sound, like the ship was being ripped apart. Icy water poured in on us from everywhere. It was like sitting beneath a waterfall.

"I heard Captain Jones yelling above the storm. 'One of the main beams holding up the deck has collapsed. We need to turn back to England, or we will drown at sea!'

"I must admit, Henry, I was in total agreement. I didn't see how we could continue with the ship falling apart all around us.

"Our leader, William Bradford, called out, 'We have committed ourselves to the will of God…we will not go back! John Howland, find a sturdy rope and meet me in the hold. We have an iron screw that we can use to secure the broken beam. We will move it from the hold and hoist it up to the deck. Hurry, lad!'

"It was very treacherous on the deck. I held on for dear life as the ship heaved back and forth. I thought we would completely tip over and be lost in the sea forever. But I obtained a strong seaworthy rope from one of the crew members and went down to the hold to help Bradford. It seemed an impossible mission.

"Bradford and I moved everything around until we found the huge iron screw. Together, we worked to move the screw up through the hatches. You can imagine what it was like, Henry, trying to work as the ship continued rolling. Many times, I thought all was lost. Finally, the screw was fixed in place, and the beam hoisted back into position.

"We praised God and sang hymns of thankfulness as the storm continued to rage outside. We had survived!"

They both became very quiet as they thought about the magnitude of the event that could have sunk the ship or sent them back to England. *I can't even imagine being tied to a post with the ocean pouring in all around. What is going to happen to me on this voyage? Is this real? Am I just dreaming? Will I ever wake up back home with the warm autumn sun and Rosie running around in the arena? Could I find the strength to be like John—to leave my family and sail away to a strange land with all the dangers and unknowns? Will I measure up?*

CHAPTER SIX

THE VAST OCEAN AND A SEA OF TROUBLES

A week had passed since he awoke on the *Mayflower* and Blake was feeling better. Aunt Ann finally freed him to work as long as he didn't overexert himself.

"Just be extra cautious for a while. If you get tired, rest!" Aunt Ann tried to give him a stern look, but ended up smiling at him. "Promise you'll be careful."

Blake gave her a hug. "I promise, Aunt Ann."

"Here's the basket. I need some supplies from the hold: dried fish, oil, biscuits and fill the jug with aqua vitae. Oh, and I need candles, too. Make sure you don't spill anything; we can't waste even a little. I hope we reach land soon. We have so little food. Will you bring some firewood, too? If the sea is calm today, I can light a fire and cook stew for dinner. And you don't need to hurry back. Humility is sleeping, so please be quiet when you return."

Blake waved at her and started toward the hold. He saw John ahead of him. "Where are you going John? I haven't seen you around lately."

John greeted his friend warmly. "I have been busy with the Carvers. Now I need to get supplies." He saw the basket and jug that Henry was carrying. "Looks like that's where you're going too."

Blake nodded and followed him down to the hold.

"John, what are you doing on this ship?" Blake was curious to know why his friend was on the *Mayflower*.

"Let's jump up onto the top of this barrel and sit. It is filled with the caulking that was used to help waterproof the ship after the mast broke." John held the lantern firmly in his hand. It was dark in the hold and very cold. "Since I'm finished with my chores until after lunch, I have time to talk. My story is a long one!

"Let me first ask if you've talked to the doctor recently? Does he think you'll regain your memory? It must be very hard to have no memory of your life before your accident on the deck." John was obviously concerned for his friend.

"He comes to see me when he is checking on others that are sick. He thinks I could regain my memory anytime, but he isn't sure because head injuries can be very hard to predict. I just have to be patient and see what happens."

Blake wondered if he would ever be able to tell John Howland the truth. *I didn't just lose my memory; I lost my whole life. I'm not really*

Henry Samson. My name is Blake James. I live in Royce County, on a ranch with my father and mother; my brother, Jackson, who loves to play football (John would not even know what football is); and my two sisters, Layla and Annie.

As the two friends talked, they could feel the forward movement of the *Mayflower*. John stared into the darkness as he started to recall his life before this journey on the *Mayflower*. "I was born in England. I left my parents and two brothers, Henry and Arthur, to come to the New World. You remind me of my younger brother." Blake smiled at him. *It's funny—John reminds me of my older brother Jackson.*

"My brothers hope to come to America once I am settled there." John continued. "We had to leave England because King James didn't like the way we chose to worship. They jailed our leaders and harassed us until we went to live in Holland. At first, we were very happy to be there because we could worship freely and openly, but whole families had to go to work to earn wages. Even the children. I was only seven years old, but I worked all day at the textile mill along with other children who were even younger than me. The Dutch were in fear of a new war with Spain, and if the Spanish won, we would be forced to leave Holland because of our faith. And after living there more than twelve years, the youngest children seemed more Dutch than English. The leaders decided to act quickly to preserve our values and secure our way of life. Our Elders decided to take our chances in the New World." John stopped to eat a bite of salted fish and drink his ale, and then resumed his story.

"We found a ship called the *Speedwell,* and in July, we boarded at the Dutch port of Delfshaven to go to England and then on to America. We were so excited to finally be on our way.

"This is a long story, is it not, Henry? I will try to tell it as quickly as I can because we will soon be missed above. But there is so much more to tell. I pray someday someone will tell this story, no matter what the outcome will be."

Blake wanted to tell him that the story of the *Mayflower* and the Pilgrims is in all the history books. Instead, he asked, "But John, why are we on the *Mayflower* and not the *Speedwell*? There's been no mention of two ships."

"When we got to the port at Southampton on the *Speedwell,* we joined up with the *Mayflower.* The plan had been to take two ships to America. But we ran into so many delays. The Merchant Adventurers Company, who were supposed to pay all our costs for this venture to the New World, changed their minds and their terms at the last minute. There was much arguing over whether we would go or stay.

"Finally, on August 5th the *Speedwell* and the *Mayflower* set sail for America. Everyone was ready to move on. After sailing about two weeks, we had just passed the chalky white cliffs of the Isle of Wight just off the coast of England. I was on the deck watching the cliffs go by. It was a beautiful day and the cliffs shone in the sun. I had never seen them before, and I was thinking I may never see them again.

"Suddenly, Captain Jones and the crew started shouting and men were climbing the masts. They were all watching the *Speedwell.* There were serious leaks in her hull, and I could see the water spewing into the ship. We had to turn into the mouth of the Dart River and sail upstream to the port of Dartmouth. We were just over a hundred nautical miles from England, and already we had to stop for repairs! When the *Speedwell* was finally repaired, we had to stay in port until the winds were favorable.

"Again, we were on our way and entered the open sea and turned westward to America. We were yet another three hundred miles on our journey when the *Speedwell*'s master signaled the *Mayflower* again. The ship had again sprung leaks even worse than before. It was either return to port or sink! So, the *Speedwell* limped back to England and we followed.

"This time we put into the port of Plymouth. There it was decided that the *Speedwell* was too unreliable for the voyage. Our leaders decided to cram as many passengers as possible on the *Mayflower* and go to America on a single ship. The *Mayflower* could not hold all the passengers, but some no longer wished to continue; all the arguing, leaks, and delays had discouraged them. It was very hard not to be discouraged. We should have been halfway through our journey to America, and now we had to begin again. We had already used up so much of our supplies. Would we have enough to reach the New World?

"And I almost forgot to mention that William Bradford heard rumors that the *Speedwell*'s master had intentionally mounted masts that were too large that would force the ship to leak at cruising speed.

That is what caused the *Speedwell* to leak and the voyage to be abandoned, therefore voiding his obligation to remain in America for a year. I heard the leaders talking about it when I was with Master Carver."

"Why would anyone do such a terrible thing?" Blake exclaimed in shock. "He put all our lives in jeopardy just for his own personal gain!"

"I have to say, Henry, I pray I am never a man like that. As for my own intentions, I do not want to stay in the New World once my four years are up. I plan to return to England and start my life there with the money I have earned."

Blake decided not to pry into John's plans, and asked instead, "How many passengers decided to make this journey?"

"There are 102 of us." They sat quietly together, thinking about the things that had happened. Blake knew the Pilgrims faced many challenges in America. *I wish I had listened better in Mr. Wilson's class. I would know what to expect if I'm still here when the ship reaches the New World.*

"Have you heard that Bill Butten is very sick with a fever?" John asked.

"I don't know if I've met him yet—at least, I don't remember him since my accident. Do you think he will get better?" Blake remembered when he was very sick with strep throat. *I went to the doctor and got medicine, but I still missed four days of school. The fever made me ache all over my body.*

"I pray he will get better," replied John. "He is getting the best care he can from Dr. Fuller. Just as I am a servant to Master John Carver and his family, Bill is the servant to Dr. Fuller. Bill is younger than you, and I've had occasion to spend time with him when both our families get together. It is one of his duties to watch the smaller children and play games with them. I would sit and listen to the men talk of religion and life in the new land. We both are very busy taking care of the family chores and running errands, so we didn't spend much spare time together. He is a likable lad. I know Dr. Fuller is very concerned for him."

"We better get back, Henry. There is still much work to do," They both slid off the barrel top and started to gather their necessary supplies. Blake followed him back up to the belly of the ship.

"Thanks for telling me all about your journey and the many harrowing things that have happened on the *Mayflower*. I hope someday I will remember it all again. Maybe I'll see you tomorrow." Blake waved as they parted ways.

Blake gave Aunt Ann the supplies that she requested. "Do you need me now?" he whispered. Blake wanted to make sure he was being useful.

"No, I don't need you now. You can come back when Humility is awake."

Blake left and took the opportunity to meet more people and see what life was really like on the *Mayflower*. He found some of the passengers had brought goats and even pigs on board, just like they had on the ranch. *No turkeys, though!* He laughed out loud thinking of the turkeys. One of the pigs just had a new litter of piglets; they were so cute and pink as they all tried to squeeze in around their mother to eat. *They are very hungry little piglets.* There were even a few chickens. He was surprised to find a cute small dog—a spaniel—and someone said there was another dog, a huge male mastiff, in one of the cabins. *I remember seeing one with my dad when we were together at an animal auction... Does he know I'm gone?*

Seeing Blake walk by, a woman stepped outside the curtain that was hanging to give a small amount of privacy to the family inside. It was similar to the tiny area that he lived in with Aunt Ann, Uncle Edward, and Humility.

"It's good to see you, Master Henry. We heard you were getting better each day. Word travels quickly here. You have not had a chance to see our new child that was born on this journey—meet our son, Oceanus Hopkins. I pray he is much calmer and quieter than this great ocean he was named for!"

Blake smiled and looked at the tiny baby held lovingly in his mother's arms. The infant started to make little sounds and then a hearty cry broke forth.

"He is hungry, and I need to feed him. Good night, Master Henry." She smiled as she closed the fabric partition.

"Good night, Mrs. Hopkins."

When Blake returned from his search, Aunt Ann was making dinner, and Humility was awake from her nap. "Will you hold Humility while I finish getting dinner ready? She wants down to play, but she isn't safe by the fire."

Blake smiled and reached for her. He sat down on a nearby stool and started to bounce her on his knee and she loved it. Her laugh was contagious and soon Aunt Ann and Blake were laughing too. It was great fun being together.

"The stew smells really good, Aunt Ann. And the fire helps to take the chill out of the air."

"Thank you, Henry. Will you please find your Uncle Edward and tell him it's time for dinner?" She gave him that special smile she seemed to save just for him. When she held out her arms, Humility went back to her.

Blake returned her smile, waved goodbye to Humility, and headed out to find his uncle to convey Aunt Ann's message. He found him with the Carvers.

"I was hoping it was getting to be time to eat," Uncle Edward said upon hearing Blake's welcomed news. "My stomach has been speaking to me in very unfriendly terms!" Everyone laughed and said goodnight.

It was cozy as they sat around the warm fire, and Aunt Ann passed each a steaming plate of stew.

Uncle Edward bowed his head over his plate. "Thank you, Lord, for this day and all your provisions. Amen."

"How was your day, Henry?" asked Uncle Edward as he took a big bite of the stew. "Has any of your memory returned?"

"My memory hasn't returned, but I spent time with John Howland today, and he explained much about the *Mayflower* and this journey. I don't understand it all, but it helps to get bits and pieces of the story. Maybe someday it will all make more sense." Blake could see that Uncle Edward was very concerned about him. *I don't know if this will ever make sense to me.*

"Even though we may not understand it, we know God has a plan for you, and it is part of His plan that you are here on the *Mayflower* with us." Uncle Edward finished his last bite. "Tomorrow is a new day. Everything is better after a good night's rest!" He stood and ruffled Blake's hair. "Let's see what the new day holds."

"Thank you Uncle Edward, and goodnight."

That night, as Blake lay in his makeshift bed, he thought about this very strange adventure that had taken over his life. He could hear everyone around him settling in for the night. Aunt Ann looked over at Blake with a smile. "Good night, Henry. God be with you."

"Good night, Aunt Ann."

He pulled the blanket up and turned on his side. While he was growing fond of his *Mayflower* family, nothing could stop the ache of homesickness that grabbed him and wouldn't let go. As the quiet tears started to flow, Blake didn't even try to stop them.

In the very early morning, Blake awoke to sounds of whispering and weeping. Someone tapped his shoulder and he turned to see John Howland's serious face.

"Henry, I wanted to be the first to tell you the news that Bill Butten died this morning."

He looked into John's eyes and saw tears streaming down his face.

"He was a good lad and I will miss him." John slipped away leaving Blake to his own thoughts and misery.

As the news spread, the passengers, who had all become like family, met in the center of the room. They prayed and thanked God for the life of Bill Butten. Dr. Fuller started to speak about the young man who had been his servant. "On this date, November 16, 1620, I give thanks for having known and cared for William. He was kind to all and always quick to give a helping hand where he could. This fever that overtook his body was more than I could minister to. I pray that the Lord will keep all our hearts in the bonds of peace and love until that time we will meet William at the very gates of heaven. It will be a joyful reunion. Amen."

Dr. Fuller turned and led the procession up the ladder, above the grates to the deck above, where William's shrouded body was lying on the deck. Everyone gathered together and sang a hymn, and then released his body into the sea.

This is too much! Too much! Blake raced down the ladder almost falling as he missed a step in his haste to get away. *Get away! Where can I go to get away? How can I get away? I miss being home. My real home.*

He headed to his mat and pulled the blanket over his head, vowing to never get up again. Just like his superhero Gaelic, he had been thrown out of his universe with a flash of lightning and he didn't know if he could find his way back. *Real death is no video game! I don't want to be here anymore. This is too real. I want to go home! NOW!*

When Aunt Ann returned to their tiny quarters after Bill Butten's funeral, she found Henry curled up and fast asleep. She knew he was struggling with the many changes in his life here and the hardships that constantly surfaced on this difficult journey. Her first instinct was to wake him and try to ease his pain, but she knew that struggles and hardships in life strengthen us, and we have to meet them face to face.

Tomorrow she would make sure he was surviving this storm.

CHAPTER SEVEN
LAND, HO!

Aunt Ann came over to Blake and touched his shoulder. She had baby Humility in her arms, and joy brightened her eyes. "Henry, Henry! Captain Jones has sent word below that they have spied land. Finally, land! We have been a long time on the sea, and there is finally land. Come, Henry! Let's go together and see what America looks like!"

Blake could feel his excitement mounting as he jumped up and started toward the deck. Everyone was hurrying to the ladder. He stopped when he saw Mr. Chilton trying to sit up on his mat.

"Master Chilton, they have spied land. Are you going to the deck?"

"Ah…Henry, I'm not sure I have the energy to climb to the deck, though it would certainly help my spirits to be able to see land after being so long in the belly of this ship!"

"Sir, I don't think I can help you to the surface by myself. I will go and find John, and he will help us." As Blake reached the deck, he saw John leaning against the rails. He had saved room for Blake and waved him over.

"Henry, how long we have been waiting for this moment!" They stood together in the early morning looking through the fog at a gray stretch of sandy cliffs and scrubby trees. It looked cold, barren, and lonely.

"So, this is what America looks like. I can't wait to get my feet on dry land again," John said.

Blake remembered why he had come in search of John. "Will you help me get Master Chilton to the deck? He is very weak, but I think it would do him good to see this for himself."

John nodded in agreement. They both went below and helped get Master Chilton to the surface and supported him by the rails.

"God bless you, lads. This is a sight for very sore bones and tired eyes!"

Standing close was one of the crew members, who Blake hadn't met. Most of the passengers didn't know the sailors, who lived and worked on the top deck. He started talking loudly, shaking his head for emphasis. "We ain't in Virginia! This is Cape Cod. We named it for all the cod fish that fill the bay. I was here in 1614 on a ship named *Elizabeth* with Captain John Smith. The storms have driven the *Mayflower* 250 miles north of our destination." There was much debating on the deck as everyone became aware of the serious problem.

"I think we best get you back to your bed, Master Chilton," said John. "I can see the fresh air and the sight of land have greatly improved your spirit. We will let you know what the outcome will be after we talk to Master Carver." John and Blake helped Mr. Chilton back below deck; it took a while to get him safely back to his bed. He gave them a weakened wave and a smile as they left, heading back up to learn what was going on.

As they stepped inside the captain's crowded cabin, they found the leaders in a heated discussion. Captain Jones was speaking. "Hear, hear! We must decide what we are going to do. As you have heard, we missed our mark and are 250 miles from our original destination at the mouth of the Hudson River. That is where we have legally been granted permission to establish a colony backed by the Merchant Adventurers. What would you have me do?"

The Pilgrim leaders conferred with each other. "We must go where we were intended to go, Captain. Turn this vessel and head south to the mouth of the Hudson River!" shouted William Bradford. Turning and seeing John behind him, Bradford directed him. "Go and tell the passengers to prepare for additional travel."

John went outside and began telling everyone in earshot that they could not stop here. "Bradford and the captain have decided we are heading 250 miles south!"

"John, how long will we have to wait to finally be at our new home?" Aunt Ann was standing among a group of her friends as she questioned him.

"It will all be according to the providence of God. Do not lose heart!"

It was cold along the coast of New England in November, but it was a clear sunny day with good winds as they steered southward. John and Blake stood on the deck watching the shoreline, staying out of the way of the busy crew. They didn't have much to say as they both were lost deep in their own thoughts.

Without warning, the *Mayflower* tilted as they hit shallow water. They could see the sand bar below the ship and the waves crashing on huge rocks near them. John and Blake held fast to the rails.

"John, I'm not sure if we're safer on the deck or below," Blake called anxiously to his friend. "We don't want to end up in the sea!" They were being tossed violently about as they looked out at the giant rocks and roaring waves.

Abruptly the winds dropped, and they could see that the *Mayflower* was in serious danger of running aground.

"We have been two long months crossing this stormy Atlantic," John replied, desperation in his voice. "I was tossed into the ocean and saved by God, with your help, my friend, and now we are going to end this voyage shipwrecked off the coast of this wilderness!"

Blake was alarmed. The mist from the sea spray was starting to soak them both. *I have never seen John so distressed.* "I think we better go below, John. Our families might need us."

They managed to make their way below deck as the *Mayflower* struggled through the rolling breakers and shallow waters. Aunt Ann was holding Humility and she was tied to a beam to keep from being tossed about. Blake went to her and watched as she lifted her voice with the Pilgrims as they sang hymns and lifted prayers for deliverance. There would be no one to rescue them if they crashed in the shallow water.

Suddenly, they felt the ship begin to turn back in the direction they had come. John and Blake ran to find Master Carver and see what was happening. They knew he would be with the other leaders and they waited for information in their usual spot in the narrow hall outside the captain's cabin.

Just as they arrived, Carver opened the door and began speaking to them. "Captain Jones has turned the ship into the wind. We must stay the night and wait for dawn. It is too dangerous to continue to the mouth of the Hudson River. We will go back to Cape Cod, where we first saw land."

At daybreak, the *Mayflower* set sail and headed back to where they had first sighted land. Blake and John met on the deck and watched the long, empty stretch of land speed by. As the sun was setting, they passed their original landfall and went a little beyond to the mainland that looked like a giant finger beckoning them to stop there. Master Jones anchored the ship for the night. The friends wished each other a good night before going to bed, and Blake spent that night trying to sleep, but instead stayed awake trying to imagine what he would find in the morning.

CHAPTER EIGHT
NEW LAND, NEW LAWS

Blake's eyes popped open. *That was a long night! I didn't think I would ever fall asleep.* He jumped up out of bed and greeted his aunt, who was already up making breakfast as Humility crawled around at her feet. "Morning, Aunt Ann. I'm hungry, but there is no way I can eat until I see what's happening above!"

She nodded with a smile. "Yes, go! Breakfast can wait!"

He moved quickly to the grate and up the ladder. The *Mayflower* was anchored in cold, calm waters. He looked around and saw John with Master Carver and a group of the leaders standing together looking out at the distant shore. Blake quickly headed over to join the group. *I can't believe I'm really here.* John saw him and made space for him in between Master Carver and Uncle Edward. Quickly the deck filled with all the passengers who were healthy enough to make it up the ladder.

William Bradford knelt down. Everyone joined him as his voice

/// 58 \\\

rang out loud and clear. "We departed England on September 16, 1620. Today, being November 11, 1620, and having arrived in a good harbor and brought safe to land, we thank the God of Heaven, who has brought us over the vast and furious ocean."

There was a loud shout of joy as the entire ship joined in the celebration.

Blake walked over to the rail where Aunt Ann stood holding baby Humility, having abandoned breakfast for this important moment. Tears were streaming down her face as she looked out at the stark and lonely shore.

"Henry, the only friends we have to welcome us are the sea gulls!" she exclaimed sadly.

The reality of the sacrifices she had made to come to this new land touched Blake's heart. She had left almost everything behind in England. Now she was facing this unknown American wilderness that would be her new home. Blake gave her a hug.

"You have changed my life, Aunt Ann. Thank you for bringing me with you and Uncle Edward. I will never forget what you have done for me, no matter what happens."

"Oh, thank you, Henry. I needed reminding that our lives are not just our own. What we do makes a difference for others, too."

He could think of no other words to comfort her.

If I ever get home again, I'm going to find you in the history books and tell everyone that you are my ancestor.

If I ever get home again.

John came over to get Blake, his face creased with concern. "Henry, the leaders and elders are all meeting in the captain's cabin to decide about the new government. Because we did not land where we were supposed to at the mouth of the Hudson River, we have no real authority to enforce and govern laws here. The contract with Merchant Adventures does not apply. Many of the men say there is no one in power over them and are talking about staging a mutiny! They say they might go their own way once we go ashore. If we don't stick together, none of us will survive! Let's see if we can find out what's going on."

When they got to the captain's cabin, many were waiting outside the door. Blake could hear the arguing and raised voices down the narrow hallway. The door finally opened, and Master Carver stood there.

"John, I need you to make a copy of this new charter, *The Mayflower Compact*! Hurry, lad."

John ran back to his quarters and grabbed his ink and quill, and then Blake followed him back inside the crowded cabin. There was a document sitting in the middle of the table.

Master Carver began to speak. "Each man must sign this Compact before anyone can set foot on land. If you cannot write, place an X and it will be legally accepted as your signature. There are nine adult males on board who cannot sign this document; some were hired as seamen only for one year, and a few are too ill to write."

Blake watched as John Carver was the first to write his name on this historical document. He then handed the quill to William Bradford. Each man in turn took the quill, wrote his name or placed an X, then handed the quill to the person next in line. When John took the quill and signed, he started to pass it to Blake.

"Henry, you are too young to sign, but you will be bound by this agreement," said Master Carver. Blake was a little disappointed. *I'm just thankful I am here to witness this. I never thought about the importance of the signing of the Mayflower Compact in American History class.* Uncle Edward looked at Blake with an understanding smile, took the quill from Stephen Hopkins and placed his signature. The last man to sign was Edward Lester. It was complete; all 41 adult men had signed it.

Carver spoke again. "This Compact is based in two principles: faith and freedom. We have stated that all source of authority is in the Name of God. Amen. And that King James holds his royal position by the grace of God. In the presence of God and one another, we have agreed to bind ourselves to establish just and equal laws for the general good of the colony."

There was a somber silence in the room.

Carver continued, "In witness, whereof we have subscribed our names at Cape Cod the 11th of November, in the reign of our Sovereign Lord King James of England, France, and Ireland, the 18th, and Scotland the 54th, Anno Domini 1620.

"Now we must elect a governor."

The men talked excitedly among themselves. Who could be trusted to hold this position? After a short period, William Bradford stood and spoke. "I choose to elect John Carver as our first governor. He has earned the reputation as a godly man and is known for his humility and leadership." There was a loud roar of approval as John Carver was chosen to lead the pilgrims in this new land.

John Carver rose, saying simply, "May God sustain me."

The door was opened, and everyone headed out. Their voices were filled with hope and excitement. They could finally move forward. William Bradford gripped John's shoulder

"John, we are headed ashore, now that the Compact has been signed. Arm yourself well, for we do not know what to expect. We know there are people native to this land, and we wish to respect them and their traditions, but we need to be prepared for every circumstance. There may be lions and tigers and bears, or God knows what else in this land.

"Master Henry, you can accompany us. We are in dire need of firewood and can use the extra hands and eyes as we search this new land. We will meet on the deck as soon as possible—go and prepare. Be quick, lad. We want to be back on board before nightfall."

Blake headed down the ladder. He was excited, but anxiety grabbed him as his stomach started doing somersaults.

"Aunt Ann, Master Bradford has asked me to join the search party going ashore! I will need some warm clothes, and I didn't eat breakfast this morning!"

"Oh, Henry, that is exciting news!" Aunt Ann exclaimed. "It is so cold—I can give you some of the clothing that I brought on the trip. And your Uncle Edward has an extra-warm coat that you can borrow to help keep you warm. I will line your own jacket with extra woolen material while you are gone. And I have been knitting a long woolen scarf on this journey; it will be perfect for you. Eat the leftovers from breakfast quickly, and I will pack a lunch to sustain you while you are with the search party."

Blake layered the clothes underneath Uncle Edward's coat. He realized how hungry he was and ate all the leftovers from breakfast. Aunt Ann handed him a cloth sack with his lunch. "Godspeed, Henry!"

He felt his heart racing as fast as his steps as he headed to the deck. He spotted John standing with the group that was going ashore. As he approached, John came and handed him a knife in a scabbard with a leather belt to secure it. "I have an extra knife that my brother gave to me. I want you to use it."

"Thanks, John! I wasn't sure what I could use."

Blake remembered the Saturday morning he and Dad had practiced knife safety. He had a really cool yellow tactical pocketknife with multiple functions—14, to be exact! What a great birthday present from his Grandma and Grandpa James. He had had to promise his mom he would always be super careful before she would even let him take it out of the box! His eyes teared up as he thought of home and his family. *I've used my knife at home to cut the twine wrapped around the hay bales. Once, I used it to carve a statue of Rosie from an old dry piece of wood I found in the barn. It didn't look like her at all. It sort of looked like a dog with a horse head. I named my wooden wonder "ROG"..."R" for Rosie... and "og" for dog. "ROG!"* Blake could picture ROG sitting on the shelf with the other collectibles in his room. Gaelic, his favorite superhero, was standing next to ROG. They made a formidable pair. Superhero Gaelic and his super mutant horse named ROG!

"Henry, are you getting ready to go?"

Blake didn't hear John; he was busy daydreaming.

Blake started to laugh out loud just thinking about ROG and Gaelic working together to rid the universe of evil forces. *If I could only get to the next level.*

"Henry! Can you hear me?"

Blake continued to stare into the distance. He didn't hear a word that John was saying.

"Henry, what is so funny?"

Suddenly, Blake was back on the *Mayflower. Oh, no! I got caught daydreaming of home. Just like I got caught daydreaming in history class.* "Sorry, John. I just had a vision of me trying to fight a bear or some wild animal. It made me laugh to even imagine it."

Whew! I need to be more careful in the future.

"Let's go, then. This is very serious, Henry. You need to concentrate on the mission. We need to be alert and not let our guard down!" John scolded Blake just like his brother Jackson would have.

"I'm ready!" Blake assured him. "Let's go."

The small workboat that had been stored on the *Mayflower* was ready and so the scouting party, led by Bradford and Captain Jones, climbed aboard and rowed to shore, aiming for the land that looked like the finger stretching into the bay.

"Henry, after being at sea more than two months, I am more than eager to set foot on dry land!" John said enthusiastically.

Blake looked at his friend and tried to hide his own fear. It didn't take long before they felt the sand rubbing up against the boat bottom. One of the men at the front of the boat jumped out and pulled it onto shore.

They stood there in a group, looking up and down the shore. It felt good to stand on land and not feel the constant sway of the boat. Blake realized how bleak and cold the landscape was.

Bradford began to speak to the group. "It is important that we all stay together and keep our eyes open to any danger. Captain John Smith was here in this area in 1614 and gathered valuable information during his trip. Smith met and traded with the many different Indian tribes and inhabitants that live here. We would like to meet them. Remember that we want to cause harm to no man. Let us head toward that forest and look for firewood."

They headed single file up the beach. Blake stayed close behind John. When they reached the coastal forest, Blake was amazed by all of the trees. *This looks so different compared to where I've lived all my life.*

Bradford had a shovel in his hand and overturned the soil in a small area close to the woods. "This black dirt is excellent and looks like it will grow fine crops. And look at all the different trees! Oaks, pines, sassafras, juniper, and so many more. Everyone grab an armload of this juniper that is on the ground. We will take it back to the *Mayflower*."

They made several trips back to the work boat until it was full. Blake's arms ached from carrying the heavy wood, but it felt good to be doing hard work. They all got into the boat and rowed back to the *Mayflower*. Together they unloaded all the wood. Everyone was eager to have firewood and warm meals to fill their bellies. That night, you could smell the sweet and strong aroma from the burning juniper. It helped cover the putrid smells that lingered from living so many months in the confined middle of the ship.

There was great joy among the passengers that night. They were ready and thankful to finally push forward to their future in this unknown land. Blake wasn't sure what he was feeling. He was exhausted from the mental and physical demands of this day. *My eyes feel so heavy, I can hardly keep them open.* As soon as his head hit the pillow, he was blissfully fast asleep, the sweet smell of the juniper weaving in and out of his dreams of his new life here, and dreams of the life he left behind.

Blake awoke to the sound of sweet singing. Aunt Ann looked

over at him and smiled.

"I didn't want to wake you. I know you were exhausted from your trip to the shore yesterday. It is so good to have firewood again. Even though our supplies are getting so low, I made you extra oatmeal. It's important you keep up your strength. Today is the Sabbath, and after service, I want you to rest. Tomorrow will be a big day. There will be more scouting out the land and trying to find food. It is a very exciting time!"

She handed baby Humility to him. "Can you watch her while I get more supplies? And I need to check on some of the sick to see if I can help them."

Blake nodded. Humility looked at him with her big blue eyes and smiled. Her hand reached out and grabbed some of the hair that was hanging above his eyes.

"Ow!"

She laughed. She looked at him like she knew who he *really* was.

"Hi there, Humility. I guess I'm your cousin, Henry." Blake put his lips close to her ears and whispered, "But my real name is Blake James, and I'm a long way from home. You're a long way from home, too. What do you think about all of this?"

She grabbed his finger and wouldn't let go. Blake looked up to see a young girl. She was the one who ran to get the doctor the day that Blake woke up on the *Mayflower*.

"Hi, Henry. Are you watching baby Humility? I am your cousin, Elizabeth Tilley. You can call me Lizzy. Ann and Edward are my aunt and uncle, too." He remembered how much she reminded him of his sister Annie. *I never thought I could miss my sister so much.*

"It's nice to officially meet you. Aunt Ann had to run an errand."

Lizzy asked, "Are you feeling better? Everyone says you lost your memory when you hit your head during the storm. Is that true?"

Blake nodded.

"I can't wait to go to the shore. I hope I can go tomorrow and help my mother wash the clothes. It's been a long time since we had clean clothes." She held out her hands to Humility and the baby went to her. "I am used to playing with the babies." Lizzy showed him how she made the baby giggle. "Just tickle her gently under the arms, Henry. It makes her laugh every time." Lizzy paused, then said, "I see you spend much of your time with John Howland."

"Yes, we are good friends."

"Does he ever talk about me?" she asked shyly.

"Yes. You should talk to him. I think you would really like him."

Lizzy looked down and blushed.

John had told Blake many times how much he liked and admired Lizzy, but Blake didn't know how to play "Cupid." He wasn't sure what he should say.

Lizzy stayed and played with the baby. Blake sat and absorbed all the sights and sounds around him. *This is where I am now. I must make the best of it. I need to help all I can—this is my family, too, after all.*

He was starting to feel more at home here.

CHAPTER NINE

NEW CHALLENGES BY THE SEA

At last! The day everyone was waiting for.
We're going ashore!

Blake rose quietly and headed to the grate. It was hard to tell what time it was because it was always dark in the middle of the ship.

On the deck, light was just starting to pierce the eastern sky. *Sunrise! I've never been on the deck to see the sunrise before. At home, I've been up early for chores or road trips, but I have never appreciated it before this moment. Everything is so quiet and peaceful and still.* The waves were quietly lapping against the ship.

He looked over to the grate as he heard approaching footsteps. "John!" His friend approached with a huge smile on his face.

"It will be a great and busy day, Henry. Master Carver said we could go ashore today and explore this new land. There is much to do to get ready. I could barely sleep last night just thinking about it.

I went to find you, but your Aunt Ann said you were gone already. I figured you would be on the deck." He paused, then mentioned, "Lizzy was there helping with Humility."

"Lizzy came over and talked with me last night," Blake told him. "She was asking questions about you!"

"Really?"

"I think she likes you. Her cheeks turn pink every time your name is mentioned!" Blake laughed.

John looked around and stammered, "I think we better get ready. They're waiting for us on the deck."

Blake just smiled at him. He could tell John was a little embarrassed and wanted to change the subject.

All around them, the activities of the crew and passengers started to pick up. Blake saw Uncle Edward standing with an animated group as they talked and anticipated the events that would mark this exciting day.

Aunt Ann hurried over to him, bouncing baby Humility on her hip. "Henry, Bradford said he saw an inlet that would be a perfect spot for our long-awaited washday. Make sure I have all your garments so I can wash them and find a place to dry and mend them. This is a much-anticipated day and will greatly improve the smell below deck! We have spent many long months cooped up below." She smiled and Humility smiled with her. "And John, I look forward to seeing Mrs. Carver on the shore and sharing this necessary but joyous task with her. Lizzy is coming to help care for the baby. Everyone is excited to be on land. Henry, would you also go to the storage in the hold and bring me up more soap? And the candles are getting low, so I will need a few more. Hurry, now. We have much to accomplish today on the new land!"

Blake went back to their tight quarters below. He started looking through his belongings and gathering up the strange clothing that he wore here. *This certainly isn't the jeans and tee shirts I wear at home.*

When he returned from the hold with the supplies, he carried the soap and dirty clothes to the deck. They would be loaded on the workboat and rowed ashore with the women.

Governor Carver approached him. "We are preparing to go ashore with Myles Standish, searching the wilderness and exploring the forest that overlooks this Cape Cod Bay. Your Uncle Edward will be coming, and he has given permission for you to accompany us. We do not know what to expect, so you need to be prepared for anything."

The next thing Blake knew, he was climbing aboard the boat that would carry them to the shore and the wilderness beyond. It took many trips in the small boat for all the eager men, women, and children to set foot on dry land after months at sea. Even some of the animals were carried and allowed to sun themselves and drink fresh water in the new land.

They all gathered together on the beach and marveled at the many wonders. Huge flocks of birds sailed in the wind and dropped down to scoop up fish. The last group to step out on the sand were the carpenters, who had with them a 35-foot longboat that was in pieces. It had been carried in sections from England, and now they were ready to repair it and use it to explore the shore of the bay. As it was unloaded, Captain Standish and the men gathered around them and the boat pieces laid out on the sand.

"Francis Eaton, you are one of the carpenters who will assemble this large sailing shallop so we will be able to explore the shore. What do you think? Will you be able to accomplish this today? We are anxious to scout this area to find food and possible lodging for the future." Captain Standish was not a large man, but he commanded respect among this company.

"Sir, this will be a much larger job than we anticipated," Eaton said. "It has been damaged during the trip. We will work very hard to get it seaworthy, but it will take much more time than we expected."

The captain nodded. "Well, men, we will explore the beach and surroundings on foot and see what we can find until the shallop is completed."

As they started down the beach, Blake looked out to the ocean and saw a huge break in the water. "Whales, sir. Look at the whales surfacing!" Blake had never seen whales in the ocean before. They all stood there marveling at the incredible sight.

Continuing onward, they saw the women and children in an inlet, scrubbing clothes on the rocks and spreading them out to dry. There was a fire to keep warm and another fire to heat the wash kettle. Just as they walked by, Aunt Ann looked up from her work and waved. Lizzy and baby Humility were playing nearby.

They explored the beach but didn't go far from the women working there. They were there to protect them from any unknown dangers until they were safely back on the *Mayflower*.

As the day wore on, they started taking turns traveling back to the ship. The women and children were first. They went back to their areas loaded with fresh, clean clothes. Tired but content, they prepared the evening meal. Now they were ready to start the next step on this journey.

That night, Blake sat with his *Mayflower* family and they ate a good, hot meal together.

Without thinking, Blake exclaimed, "This reminds me of the stew my mother makes!" His jaw dropped open. *I can't believe I said that out loud!*

"Henry, is your memory coming back?" Aunt Ann gasped, overjoyed. "Your mother is a good cook, and I always loved her stew, too. Maybe you are starting to remember again!"

"The words just came out of my mouth. I'm not sure I remember anything else," Blake stammered.

"Don't worry about it, Henry. It will happen when and if it's supposed to happen. You have been getting along just fine. Don't lose heart." Uncle Edward put his hand on Blake's shoulder. "We will be here for you either way."

"Thank you both. We will take care of each other, no matter what," Blake agreed.

The Tilley's talked about their worries and the dwindling food supplies. What would they find at the end of each new day? What about the Native Americans that lived on this land? Would the new settlers be able to live in peace with them? Would they find food?

Blake just sat and listened. *This is what family does. It doesn't matter if I'm on the Mayflower, or back home. We will take care of each other.*

CHAPTER TEN

SEARCHING FOR NEW NEIGHBORS

In the morning, Blake woke as John tapped him on the shoulder and pointed up to the deck. They both went up and joined the group of men that gathered, John turning to Blake as they did so. "Henry, Captain Standish is going on another expedition and has asked us to go. He plans to survey the area in more detail. We need to gather supplies and prepare to go as soon as possible." Blake could almost feel the excitement in John's voice.

Blake headed below and found Aunt Ann to tell her about the new expedition, and she began preparing a food sack for him.

"Go below and get more aqua vitae," she told him. "Make sure you dress in warm clothes, and don't forget the knife that John gave you." Blake hurried and got ready for the journey, eating the leftover stew from last night after finishing his preparations.

As he rose to leave, Aunt Ann handed him the food and gave him a hug. "Godspeed, Henry."

It took two trips in the small boat to get the 16 men to shore. They began exploring in a single file formation, with Blake and John in the middle. It was difficult walking through the sand. Many in the group had firearms, swords, and the heavy body armor they brought from England.

They had barely marched a mile when they saw a small party of six or seven Indians heading their way. There was a dog trailing behind. As soon as they saw the Englishmen, the party fled into the forest. Blake was both excited and nervous to see them.

"Men, I am hoping to talk with them. Let's follow and catch up with them if we can." As soon as he gave the order, Captain Standish led the group into the woods. They followed the Indians' tracks all day. When it became dark, they stopped to camp overnight in the woods. "We will post guards tonight and resume the trail in the morning," Standish decided.

John and Blake sat down on a log after gathering firewood; they were both exhausted from walking all day. It felt good to sit close to the fire. It was dark and cold, and many strange sounds were heard around them. Together, they drank their aqua vitae and got out their bag of food. The biscuit and cheese never tasted so good. *I wish there was more to eat.*

He remembered when his family had taken a trail ride into the woods on their ranch. He was riding his horse, Rosie, and they had stopped and camped by a stream. After eating roasted hot dogs and marshmallows, they told scary stories by the fire. *There were strange night sounds there, too.*

He looked up through an opening in the trees and saw the stars above. *These are the same stars I see at home.* It soothed his fears and homesickness. He could hear two owls off in the distance calling to each other. It was such an eerie sound. Could the owls actually be the party of the Indians they had been following? He knew they could mimic birds and animals and use them to communicate to each other. *I can mimic turkeys. Not sure it will help much here, though.* He had to smile a little as he thought of his history class, the squirming beetle, and his turkey dance. *It all seems so long ago.*

"What do you think about this day, John?" Blake asked his friend. "Did you see when the Indians stepped into the woods? Do you think we will find them tomorrow?"

"I hope we meet them soon. We had heard many stories before we set off from England about the people that live in this land. We have hoped to meet the natives and greet them peaceably. We are expecting the blessing of God in this land, and he expects us to treat all with honor and respect. Our difficulties may be many, but not invincible."

Blake was happy that he had met John Howland and they were friends. He was learning so much about facing fears and doing what was good and honorable. *I don't need my superhero Gaelic when I have a true friend in John. Although I do need ROG! Ha!*

At the break of dawn, they continued their search. They pushed through dense thickets that tore at their clothes and skin. Marching through boughs and bushes, over hills and into valleys, the group still found there was no trace of the natives. When the supply of aqua vitae was gone later that morning, the need for fresh water was vital.

"I'm so thirsty, my tongue is sticking to the roof of my mouth!" It was hard for Blake not to complain too much.

At about ten o'clock, they finally found springs of fresh water and decided it was the best water anyone had ever tasted. *This is the first real water I've had since leaving home*, Blake realized. Captain Standish made a fire to signal to the ship, so they knew where the group was located. Continuing, they found a pond of fresh water that had ducks and vines and sassafras.

Everyone was getting tired, and some of the men lagged. Down a path were mounds of sand covered with mats. Upon closer inspection, they were thought to be graves. Everything was left untouched out of respect and they marched on.

They found walnut trees full of nuts and berries that were eaten with great joy. It was the first fresh fruit anyone had eaten in a long time. Onward they marched, finding wooden planks from an old house. There, sitting in middle of an old fire pit, was a great iron kettle! The men close to Blake said it came from some ship brought out of Europe.

Captain Standish kneeled to examine a heap of sand, which he dug up and found an old basket full of Indian corn. He placed guards around them as they examined the basket: 36 ears of corn were inside the round basket that was narrow at the top. The corn—red, yellow, and some mixed with blue—spilled from the opening as they lifted the heavy treasure from the sand.

"Look how beautiful and intricate this basket is! But how can we just take what doesn't belong to us? Is this morally acceptable?" asked Standish.

There was much discussion before they decided on a compromise: being short of food, they would take the iron pot and corn, and once they met the Indians, they would return the pot and pay them for the corn.

John looked at Blake and nodded in agreement. They filled their pockets with as much corn as they could carry, and two men carried the pot full of loose corn on a wooden pole between them. The rest of the corn was reburied.

That evening, after additional exploration, they went back to the freshwater pond and camped for the night. There was a great fire, and three men took turns watching the camp and keeping the fire going. It was wonderful—until the rains came. And then things quickly became miserable.

"I know you're wet and cold, but try to get some sleep. We don't know what to expect for tomorrow. I'm sure we'll need all the energy we can muster." John was taking care of Blake just like his brother Jackson would if he were there. Blake lay there as the rain pounded on him. His thoughts found their way home. He could see his family out in the distance and hear the rain dancing on the metal roof of the barn. It was soothing. He thought he could hear Rosie and Ben out playing in the rain.

Finally, sleep found him.

Everything was soaking wet when morning came. Even the cast iron pot was mired in the mud. The men were busy cleaning and drying their muskets, for they wouldn't fire when wet. John had a gun with him, but Blake had only his knife, which he pulled out to dry the sheath close to the fire. It was so cold and wet, and he didn't leave his spot on the log. He knew he would warm up once they started to march. He thought of all the times he had complained about doing his chores at home. *Here we have very little to eat and little time to rest. This expedition is exhausting.*

Once again, they set off searching the wilderness. Blake stayed right behind John in single file. Ahead, everyone stopped when they came to a peculiarly bent young sapling, with some acorns at its base. While they were looking at it, William Bradford came up unintentionally from the rear and accidentally stepped on it. It gave a sudden jerk up and caught his leg. Bradford wasn't hurt or alarmed, but everyone was curious and amazed at the clever trap that must have been set by the Indians to snare game.

As they marched on, they saw great flocks of wild geese and ducks, and high above the creek were three bucks peering down at the group. They looked so regal and strong. Weary from their exploration, they arrived back at the beach just before sundown. The men were bursting with tales of all they had seen.

Later that evening, Blake told Aunt Ann all about it. "As we marched, we had no idea where we were until we reached the shore. Thank God Captain Jones and Master Carver had the signal fires going, or we may have wandered into the night. It was so good to see the shallop and *Mayflower* waiting for us in the bay."

The search continued for weeks to find a suitable location for the colony; sometimes Blake would be asked to join them, but other times he stayed on the ship. They were now getting extremely low on food.

Blake was on deck when he saw Uncle Edward return from the six-day expedition led by Captain Jones. Uncle Edward immediately went below deck and Blake followed him to their shelter. He looked tired and sick and had a deep cough. Blake could see the deep concern for him that instantly clouded Aunt Ann's face.

Many of the passengers, hearing that he was back, came and gathered around. They were all anxious to hear news.

"It was Wednesday, December 6th that we set out with 10 men searching for a good location for the new colony." Despite his fatigue and illness, Uncle Edward was anxious to tell everyone the details of what had become a near-fatal expedition. "We rowed the boat along the coastline trying to find smoother water so we could hoist our sails. After traveling for six or seven hours by the shore, we still saw no river nor shore with a sandy point. The gunner and I became very sick, and I had fainted with the cold. The water froze on our clothes and made like several coats of iron. As we prepared to beach the shallop, we saw a group of Indians farther down the shore crowding around a large object on the edge of the bay. We didn't want to make contact, so we posted guards and camped for the night. We made a barricade, got firewood, and set our guards. About four or five miles from us, we saw the smoke of the fire the natives made that night.

"In the morning, we divided our company—eight went to the shallop, and the rest of us went to discover this new land. It was only a bay without a river or creek coming into it. We also found a large whale dead on the sand. The men in the shallop found another two dead at the bottom of the bay. It seems they had been trapped because of the frost and ice and could not return to the ocean. We did not have the means or the time to take them back for food. So, those of us who had not been in the shallop rejoined the others, and we continued to search the beach.

"We found the place where the Indians had their fire the night before. They had been cutting up a whale, and in their haste to leave had dropped scattered pieces by the way. We followed their foot-prints up the sands and into the woods. We scouted all day, but we found no suitable location for the colony nor another sign of the Indians. We stopped and built a makeshift fort out of logs and brush, posted guards, and built a large fire. We were both faint and weary, for we had eaten nothing all day. Here we slept for the night until we were awakened by wolves making hideous cries. We later found it was not wolves, but instead Indian war cries."

Uncle Edward stopped talking as Aunt Ann brought him a warm drink and tucked another blanket around his shoulders. It was obvious this trip had taken a great toll on him. He looked around the group and continued his tale.

"The next day, we were attacked. Some of the men had carelessly left firearms on the shore by the beached shallop, and the natives tried to capture our weapons. We found ourselves in a volley of arrows. Our men ran with great speed to recover our weapons, and they did. There were only four of us ready to defend the boat. We thought it best to defend it rather than lose all our things. Captain Standish got a couple shots off.

"One of our men, wanting to discourage our enemy, pulled a huge log out of the fire and ran into them. It didn't stop them at all. Their cries were dreadful. I looked into the woods and saw a very distinguished man standing behind a tree. I believe he was their leader. He shot three arrows at us and we returned fire. He let out an extraordinary cry, and away they all went. We left six men at the shallop and followed them about a quarter of a mile. We did this that they might see we were not afraid of them, nor discouraged."

Uncle Edward stopped, took a slow sip of his drink, and started again.

"In the dark of morning, we could not see the natives among the trees, but they could see us by our fire. When it was light, we gathered up 18 of their arrows to send back with Captain Jones to

England. Many across the sea would be excited and want to see and examine them. Some of the arrows were headed with brass, deer horn, or eagles' claws. Many of the arrows had come close to us. As we searched, we saw more of the arrows were all around us. Some of our coats which hung by our barricade were shot through and through, but their arrows neither hit us nor hurt us."

Uncle Edward stopped for a moment and pulled something from his pocket. "I saved several of the arrowheads so you could see them with your own eyes." He passed them one by one to Blake, who was sitting right beside him. He studied each one, then passed them around to the group.

Continuing, Uncle Edward said, "After we had given God thanks for our deliverance, we took the shallop and continued on our journey. We sailed westward exploring Cape Cod Bay's southern shoreline. After a couple hours, we were miserable as we were pelted with snow and rain. The seas began to roll in large waves, and we realized we were in the midst of a heavy gale and in great danger again. Our small ship was starting to come apart at its seams; it was not holding up to the ferocity of the storm. And we were thinking, 'had we just survived the attack by the natives only to be killed by wind and waves?' Suddenly, the storm pushed our boat straight onto a stretch of sandy beach. There we built a bonfire to combat the cold and spent the night.

"The next morning was Saturday, December 9th. We realized we were on a forested island. The storm had passed, the sun appeared, and we remained on the island. We stayed all day drying our weapons and equipment and repairing the shallop. We spent the night and, as the following day was the Sabbath, worshipped and rested during the day.

"Let me tell you, my dear family and friends, that on the next day, Monday, December 11th, we found the location for our colony."

Aunt Ann grabbed his hand and let out a gasp of joy. "Edward, could this really be true? Have you found the location we have been praying for?"

Edward looked at her with great love and kindness. "Yes, Ann. We found the location. It was like the hand of God directed us right to it.

"We arose in the morning and sailed westward from the island into a broad, sheltered harbor. On a high hill above the harbor was a site that had been cleared of timber. There were no signs of the natives anywhere, but we are sure they had cleared this land. There were only empty, abandoned cornfields. We walked the grounds of this huge clearing. Along the base of the hill ran a very sweet brook that emptied into a salt marsh. The ground was good and was composed of rich, black earth. We found the harbor will accommodate the *Mayflower* and fishing for cod. We will not have to spend countless man hours to clear this site, although we'll have to walk a far distance to cut firewood and logs for building. And the site is a perfect location to defend ourselves with an unobscured view of the bay. If we all approve this site, we can begin building our homes here."

A cheer went up among the group. "It will be good to build our homes and start our new life here. Finally, we will have a place to live that doesn't rock us to sleep at night!" Aunt Ann spoke next. "Sadly, we have bad news to share. I'm sorry to tell you, Edward, that while you were on the expedition with Master Bradford, his sweet wife Dorothy fell from the ship and drowned. Into the icy waters she slipped, and no one was able to save her. It is dreadful news for Master Bradford. As we all knew, she was just 23. They left their three-year-old son, John, in England until they were settled here and could send for him."

Uncle Edward looked shocked as the news touched his heart. "It seems somehow wrong to celebrate when such a terrible tragedy has touched our own William Bradford," he said softly.

Quiet weeping could be heard as the weary passengers remembered the young woman who had been part of their lives these months and endured the same trials, only to fall into the sea and drown.

The small group headed back to their own partitions. It was a long day, and they all had much to talk about. The excitement of finding the location of their colony, the trepidation of the hardships that faced them, and the loss of one of their own would be the focus of many conversations tonight.

It was dinner time, and Aunt Ann needed to take extra care with Uncle Edward, who was exhausted from the trip, the storytelling, and the dreadful news about Dorothy Bradford. She heated the blankets by the stove and helped him undress and stretch out on the small cot. When the stew was ready, she added more broth to it and fed him spoonfuls.

"Thank you, Ann," Uncle Edward said wearily. "I know if I have a good night's rest, I will be better in the morning."

She smiled at him and gently tucked the blankets around him. "I need to get Humility from Lizzy. She is caring for her while she took her nap."

When she left, Uncle Edward called Blake over to him. "Henry, I did not allow you to go on this expedition because you need to stay healthy. I know you were disappointed, but you will have plenty of time to explore and build homes. Captain Jones has given us permission to live on the *Mayflower* until we have found that exact location and build our lodgings. He cannot feed us from the ships' rations any longer, for he will need those to return to England when the time comes."

Blake shook his head as he understood the severity of his words and concern for his safety.

Uncle Edward continued, "I want you to take care of your Aunt Ann and Humility, if anything should happen to me." He started coughing and had to wait to continue. "You are a good lad and I am glad we brought you on this trip. I have seen the care and love you have shown, thinking of others before yourself."

Seeing his uncle's exhaustion, Blake said, "Please rest, Uncle Edward. I promise to do my best to take care of all of you! If something should happen, I will not fail you or Aunt Ann and baby Humility."

Uncle Edward nodded, then laid back down and closed his eyes.

That night, Blake earnestly said his prayers. He thought of home and wondered how he could keep his promise to Uncle Edward. He had never thought about death much before he woke up on the *Mayflower*. Once one of their young calves on the ranch died, and everyone was sad. *This is so different. I was overwhelmed when Bill Butten died here, but I didn't know him. And now Uncle Edward seems so sick!*

Blake's turmoil kept him awake into the night.

What will I do?

CHAPTER ELEVEN
A LAND OF PROMISE

About a week after the expedition returned, Captain Jones set sail for the western shoreline to explore the new colony site. Once again, Blake and John met on the deck and excitedly talked about building the homes and exploring the area together. It was about 30 miles from where they had previously been anchored. Blake was anxious to get started.

The next day, they reached their new destination and Captain Jones anchored the ship in the bay. Blake couldn't wait to find John and get started. They had not been part of the expedition that had found the site and they were anxious to explore. Soon the shallop landed on the beach, and everyone walked up the hill and started hiking the grounds of the sprawling clearing. Almost everyone agreed there was much to like about the site. As Uncle Edward had said, drinking water was accessible and there was easy access to the bay for fishing.

Some people standing around, however, were mumbling and talking among themselves. Finally, one called out, "Governor Carver, we are not sure this is the best location to start our colony. We think we should continue to look before we make such an important decision!"

Carver considered what they had to say before speaking. "I think we need to pray and remember what we are up against. Many of our people are ill, and we can't delay much longer. It's important to get the buildings raised and think about planting crops in the spring. We are very low on food, and here we could fish and hunt to provide sustenance for everyone. We have just started to see the reality of the harsh winters here. Captain Jones has agreed to let us live on the *Mayflower* until our houses are built, but he can stay only a few more months before he heads back to England. Of course, we wish everyone could agree, but we will have to go along with the majority when we vote and make decisions."

Everyone continued to walk about the huge clearing and tried to imagine what home would be like here.

John turned to Blake. "I wonder what happened to the people who once lived here. There was obviously a lot of work done to make this clearing. Where did they go? It looks like it has been abandoned for a while."

"You're right, John. And it doesn't look like they are coming back!"

They both stood there taking in the scenery.

Finally, John spoke. "I believe this will be a good place to live. I have been on that ship long enough, and I'm ready to start building. We will have to walk a distance to fell the trees, but there is much material available to gather for the thatched roofs."

Blake agreed.

Off in the distance, they could see the tree line of the forest. It was a cold, sunny day, and Blake felt the sudden urge to run like he used to run in the pastures at home.

"I'll race you to the trees!" He took off running across the clearing. Suddenly, it felt like he was back home in Royce County, racing Jackson through the grasses and dusty paths on their ranch. Faster and faster he ran. Maybe if he ran fast enough, he could be back home. *Home!* His lungs were burning as he flew across the field. He turned to see if it was his brother, Jackson, whose feet were pounding the ground behind him. It wasn't Jackson, but his good friend, John—John Howland from his history book. He stopped when he reached the tree.

They looked at each other and started laughing. It felt good to laugh and feel young again. *Everything is so hard here.* They both took a minute to catch their breath. Off in the distance, some of the animated group started back down the hill, to the shore, and the workboat that would take them back to the *Mayflower*. There, they would vote and decide if this would be the site of their new home.

"I think we are both going to feel this tomorrow, but it felt so good to be free of the ship and our cares!" John said, looking over at Blake and rubbing the muscles in his legs. As they were preparing to go back, they heard a slight rustle in the brush just inside the trees. They looked up to see a young Indian sitting on a beautiful spotted pony with a deer tied on the pony's back. He didn't seem much older than Blake. Even though his face was painted with bright colors, he was camouflaged and well hidden within the trees. The three of them studied each other, John and Blake caught by surprise. The moment seemed frozen in time. No one moved at first.

Slowly, the Indian boy turned his pony and headed back into the woods.

"Henry, we must never leave the group without weapons again," John said after the boy left. "I think he was as curious about us as we were about him. I felt no harm from him, but we need to be more careful in the future."

They set off to catch up with the group, share what they had seen, and row back to the *Mayflower*. They were in this new land that was full of unknowns. They both knew they needed to be more careful.

"Governor Carver! We just saw a young Indian in the woods!" John pointed to the tree line where they saw him. "It looked like he had been hunting, for there was a deer on the pony's back. He seemed very curious about us, as we were with him. After a moment, he turned and headed back into the woods!"

Carver glanced at the tree line with concern before turning back to John, his concern turning to thoughtfulness. "That is good to know, John. I'm sure he will be telling his leaders about the encounter. They

will know we are here. Maybe we can meet with them in the future. They can watch us and see our intentions are honorable. And we can keep watch to make sure their actions are honorable, too."

With that said, Carver and the group headed back to the *Mayflower*.

That night, Blake laid down with the vision of the young Indian sitting on the beautiful spotted pony. Blake could still see his painted face and the long braids that hung down below his shoulders. Two beautiful white feathers were tied at the back of his head. *I wonder if he is thinking of us, too.*

His thoughts turning homeward, Blake whispered as he was falling asleep, "Don't forget me, Rosie. As soon as I get back, I'll take you for that ride I promised you."

———————

For the next week, everyone was stuck inside as gale-force winds and rains pounded the ship. People were getting stir-crazy. They had voted to accept the site of the colony. Not everyone had agreed, but once the vote was counted, they all wanted to move forward. How can you move forward when you can't get off the ship? How can you build houses if it rains all the time?

Uncle Edward's cough wasn't improving, and Dr. Fuller came often to see him.

Sometimes, when John was free, he came and sat with them. Lizzy would come over to play with Humility. She was always cheerful and was the first to step in and take care of her family when needed. He knew how much she loved playing with Humility and cared for the other children on board. When they were all together, Blake often saw John and Lizzy smile shyly at each other as their eyes met. John told him once that he hoped to marry Lizzy one day.

There were some girls in Blake's classes that he liked, but he was too embarrassed to tell them. *And I'm NOT ready to think about marrying anyone!* He thought about the turkey day in history class and how much he liked to show off for Sarah. She only seemed annoyed when he was around! He really didn't understand how to get girls to like him. *I always end up saying stupid things. I don't think I'll ever get married. Maybe I'll just live on the ranch with Mom and Dad forever. I'm sure they can use my help.*

Finally, the rain and wind stopped! All the able-bodied headed back to the site and to the woods to start cutting down trees, the same area where John and Blake had seen the Indian boy on the spotted pony. There was a steady rhythm of axes chopping wood and trees falling as men called out a warning before they hit the ground.

Their first task was to build a "common house" for storage, protection, and temporary shelter as needed. All the timber had to be hauled back to the site and split into rough planks. It was back-breaking work. Once the common house was built, they would start building individual homes, which would all be topped with a thatched roof. It was agreed that families would have top priority in housing, and that the single men would live with a family until more houses could be erected later for them.

Plans were made to bring a cannon from the *Mayflower* to the site in order to protect the fields over the land and the shoreline and harbor. There would be a special house for the governor and Myles Standish near the crest of the hill. The town was planned with houses to be built on both sides of a narrow street that extended up the hill.

The plans were made, and now the hard work would keep them busy for months. *Months? Will I really be here for months? Am I really here now? What is happening at home on the ranch? Does anyone miss me yet? Am I just dreaming?* As Blake pondered all these things, his heart sank.

"This is too freezing cold to be a dream!" His breath frosted as he spoke.

CHAPTER TWELVE

THE SPECIAL CHRISTMAS GIFT

On Monday, Blake awoke as Aunt Ann touched his shoulder and whispered "Merry Christmas, Henry! We are very blessed to remember the birth of Jesus here on the *Mayflower*."

Blake sat up. "Christmas? Merry Christmas, Aunt Ann." Blake immediately felt a stab of homesickness. His mom would be up early baking her special cinnamon rolls. They were amazing and the smell filled the whole house. It had been a James' family tradition for as long as he could remember. Dad would build a fire in the fireplace, put on the Christmas music, and everyone would come down to breakfast in pajamas. Thinking about his home made him wonder if Aunt Ann felt the same. "We had to leave our homes behind. Does that make you sad, Aunt Ann?"

"Even Mary and Joseph had to leave their home and travel many miles alone. I bet they were cold, tired, and frightened just as we are at times. But our heavenly Father had a plan for them, just as he does for us, too. We must trust Him just as Mary and Joseph trusted Him. Can you imagine the sound of all the angels singing when Jesus was born? 'Glory to God in the highest, and on earth, peace and goodwill toward men.' To think that tiny baby born is the Son of God.

"Your Uncle Edward and I were never blessed with our own children, but we have been blessed to have you and Humility to love and care for."

Blake gave her a puzzled look.

Aunt Ann smiled and explained, "Humility's father is my brother, Robert Cooper. His wife, Joan, died in childbirth and Robert was not able to care for her by himself. We decided to bring her with us and raise her in America.

"Henry, your dear mother is my sister, Martha. Your father is James Samson. I hope someday when your memory returns, you know what wonderful people they are. They were very distressed to send you away, but you wanted to come with us to the New World. They wanted you to have every opportunity for a good life here, so they agreed to let you come in our care.

"I'm reminding you of this today because I have something for you. They didn't want you to come here penniless. I promised them I would give this to you on your first Christmas here. Merry Christmas, Henry, from your mother and father in England," Aunt Ann reached in her pocket and handed him a small leather pouch. When Blake looked inside, he could barely breathe. *This is the same coin I found hidden in the desk drawer!*

"Henry, what is wrong? Is your memory returning? You look so pale. Have you suddenly remembered your parents? The doctor said your memory could return at any time."

Blake was so overcome by the gift of the coin that he could not speak. *THE COIN!* The same mysterious coin that had started this dream, or whatever this was that was happening to him. He wished he could tell Aunt Ann about the coin, the hayloft, his family. But he just sat there, stunned. Finally, he managed to say, "Thank you, Aunt Ann. I'm not sure what I'm feeling. My parents must be remembering me today, and their gift of the coin. Could you tell me whose face is on the coin?"

"Certainly, Henry! It's King James!"

Blake remembered looking at the coin in the hayloft. He had been trying to recognize the silhouette when he first found it, but he had no idea it was King James. He was amazed to think the coin had been passed down through all the generations starting with Henry. *From Henry Samson, December 25, 1620, to Blake James.*

Now, maybe I can go home again. But how...how can I get home again?

At that moment, he could hear John Howland making his way to their partition. He always spoke to everyone along the way: "Tis wonderful to wake up this Christmas Day, knowing God has directed our path to this new land. We can give Him glory and honor by working hard on our new colony—Plymouth Colony."

Blake saw John give a quick smile and greeting to Lizzy Tilley as he passed by her. She waved and smiled back. Quickly, Blake slid the coin, still wrapped in its leather pouch, into his pocket.

"Good morning and Merry Christmas, Mistress Ann." John gave her a huge grin.

"Thank you, John, and a blessed and Merry Christmas to you," Aunt Ann said warmly.

"Henry, the workboat is ready to take us to shore," John said. "We need to continue cutting the trees and hauling them to the building site. No time to rest today."

Blake nodded and grabbed the food sack Aunt Ann had prepared the night before. He turned back to face her, and asked, "Is there something special I can do? I have no gifts for you, Uncle Edward, or Humility. I wish I had something special for you."

"Go and work hard building us all a home. That is the best gift you could give!"

He gave her a hug and followed John to the deck.

Upon reaching shore, they walked to the clearing on the hill, and then headed to the woods. There they were divided into three groups. The first group cut trees, the second split logs in the direction of the long fibers, and the third carried them to the site. Blake was part of the third group that carried the wood and stacked it at the edge of the location. All day they worked, stopping only long enough to eat their lunches. Blake and John sat on the edge of one of the logs as they ate. The smell of the sea combined with the fresh-cut lumber and wet earth filled up their senses. It had a wonderful, spicy, pungent smell. Above, the clouds were starting to turn gray.

"We better get back to work," John advised, glancing up at the sky. "Looks like rain might be headed our way."

John was right. The winds picked up and they hurried their pace. Bradford called to everyone to finish what they were doing and hurry to shore. There was a storm brewing, and they didn't want to get caught in it. Twenty of the men stayed ashore to keep guard and the rest climbed into the workboat. Just as they reached the ship, large drops of rain started falling, sending everyone below deck.

That night, they celebrated Christmas with meager supplies but thankful hearts. Blake thought once more of Christmas at home: a decorated tree, the smell of fresh pine, and cookies galore with presents under the tree. Everyone was always excited to see what special surprise was hidden inside the bright wrapping paper on gifts that had their name on them. He felt his pocket and the small pouch that held the coin. *Of all the Christmas gifts I have received, I will never forget this one. What will I do with it? Will it help me get home again?*

CHAPTER THIRTEEN

NEW YEAR, MORE SICKNESS

There had been only one day the men could work on the colony as the foul weather continued after Christmas and into the start of the new year. As they gathered thatch for the roofs, they saw great Indian fires. Captain Standish and four other men tried to meet them, but they stayed hidden. When the weather finally improved, the settlers started building the town once again. The common house was almost finished, but it still needed its thatched roof. Blake walked the inside of the building. It was about 20 square feet. *This is about the size of our hayloft where I found the coin.*

Some of the workers were making mortar and others continued to gather thatch. Blake liked to make the mortar, a task that involved mixing dirt with grass and water to make a thick paste. By the end of the week, he was also gathering thatch. John was cutting down trees. At lunch, they sat together and watched two of their company, John Goodman and Peter Brown, head deeper in the woods with their two dogs. Seeing the dogs always made Blake's heart ache for his family and home. Their dogs were always the first to greet you when you came home. Quickly, he felt in his pocket for the pouched coin. It was still there. When it started to rain, they both went to the common house to stay dry. Thankfully, the thatched roof had been completed.

"Henry, you seem to be off in your own world lately," John observed. "Are you okay? Is there something that is bothering you? I know I am worried about all the sickness, and we have had 12 of our people die so far—William Bradford is sick here now, too. Maybe it will get better when we get the houses built and everyone can move from the *Mayflower* into the town. The weather was never this cold in England."

They both sat in the far corner of the common house, waiting for the rain to stop. The heavy rain sloshed in under the door and the floor was wet mud. It was miserable.

"I'm okay," Blake said eventually. "I do worry about Uncle Edward. He hasn't gotten much better after experiencing the bitter cold expedition in December. That was almost a month ago. He asked me to take care of Aunt Ann and Humility if anything happens to him." Blake was quiet for a moment. He wished he could tell John everything. "And Aunt Ann gave me a coin that was a Christmas gift from my parents in England. I don't remember them, but I do have the coin. Maybe someday I will remember everything that has happened to me." *Will I ever understand this? Will the coin be able to take me back? And how?* These thoughts were always in Blake's mind.

"We need to just keep pushing forward and do the best we can do. I will be glad when we have the houses ready and we can plant in the spring." John was good at bringing the focus back to building the colony.

When it was time for dinner, several of the men came over to John and Blake. Worry was evident in their faces and posture.

"John Goodman and Peter Brown and their dogs haven't returned from the woods," one of the men told them. "They went looking for more material to make the thatch. We went to look for them, but have found no sign of them. We are worried because we have seen the Indian fires. It is too late and dark now, but tomorrow we'll start looking for them again. Be prepared in the morning to help us search!"

The friends both ate their thin soup, biscuits, and some salted cod and found a spot to sleep for the night. Blake felt the coin in his pocket. The coin and his promise to Uncle Edward were weighing heavy on his mind. If he tried to leave now, it would be a betrayal to all who needed him here. *I have to stay positive. I can't start feeling sorry for myself.* He remembered his conversation with his father.

"Life is too short to waste it feeling sorry for yourself, Blake. My attitude affects me and everyone around me, so I choose to stay positive. You have to keep working at it."

I promise that I'm doing my best, Dad. I won't fail. I'll make you and

Uncle Edward proud of me.

A peace settled over Blake, a peace he hadn't felt in a long time. He knew what the right answer was. He had to stay until he knew for sure it was time to go. He hadn't really found the coin; the coin had found him. First in the hayloft, then on the *Mayflower*. Maybe the coin would take him home again when the moment was right.

In the morning, they left with eight others to search for the missing men. They walked and called out for them all day. It had started to snow and freeze by the time they turned back. Exhausted and worried, they began to think the natives must have surprised and captured Goodman and Brown.

As they settled into the common house, they heard dogs continuously barking outside. Everyone stepped outside to see the lost men returning with their dogs. They could barely walk, and several men ran to help them. Once inside, the group gathered around the weary and famished men. Blake filled a bowl with the warm soup and started to feed Peter Brown. John Goodman pointed to his feet, pleading, "Please help me, I think my feet are frozen in my boots!"

John Howland looked and tried to remove the boots, but Goodman's feet were swollen inside. Blake handed him his sharp knife and John started cutting away the frozen boot.

Finally, Goodman's feet were freed, and he tried to move closer to the fire, obviously in great pain.

One of the men called out a warning: "Don't get your feet too close to the fire. They need to thaw slowly."

"Where have you been? We searched two days for you," said Master Leaver, who had been the first to notice they were missing. "We thought the natives had found you."

It was Peter Brown who spoke first. "We took the dogs and started looking deeper in the woods for more thatch. We found a lake where there was a great deer. The dogs took off chasing it, and we found ourselves lost because we went after the dogs and couldn't find our way back. It started raining, and that night it did freeze and snow. We had no weapons or food and tried to sleep on the ground covered with leaves for warmth.

"We heard two wild beasts roaring and a third off in the distance. They sounded like lions. We had to grab and hold tight to the dogs, for they wanted to take after them. We didn't know what to do, so we tried to climb a tree to find safety, but it was too cold, and we thought the beasts might follow us up the tree. But it pleased God that they did not follow us. It was extremely cold, and we walked back and forth under the tree all night.

"As soon as it was light, we started looking for the way back. Finally, we walked to a high hill and saw the familiar two isles in the bay. We knew our way to the colony from there. We traveled all day and were both ready to faint when we finally arrived in the area. The dogs started to bark, knowing we were close to home."

Everyone in the common house slept better that night knowing the lost had been found. They could take nothing for granted in this new land. After this harrowing experience, no one wandered off again.

The next day, a strong wind swept up the hill. William Bradford was still sick in bed, along with Governor Carver, who had recently fallen ill. Outside, a spark from the fire landed on the newly thatched roof of the common house. It didn't take long for the fire to sweep across the thatch and quickly destroy the whole roof, even though everything was saturated from the rain. Blake was closest to the door and went running to help the two sick men get outside. Thankfully, there was no major harm done to anyone, or to the common house. They could waste no time and started immediately to attach new thatch to the roof.

"What next?" Blake said aloud. The wind caught his words and sent them spinning around before anyone heard them. He felt the weight of the coin in his pocket and on his heart. *What next?* He didn't have a clue, but whatever challenge they faced next, he would give it his best. That's all he could do.

―――――――――

Blake, John, and all the able-bodied men worked hard to build the cottages after repairing the common house's roof. Of the 19 cottages that had been planned, only seven had been built by spring. Captain Jones needed to prepare to sail back to England and wanted the sick off the *Mayflower*. Half of his men had died from illness, and he didn't want any more of them exposed to the illnesses that were still rampant among the settlers.

John and Blake boarded the shallop and headed back to the ship. Blake was anxious to see Aunt Ann, Uncle Edward, and Humility again, as he had stayed on shore for weeks to help get the buildings ready while they remained aboard the ship. John went to find the Carver family, and Blake made his way to the familiar place below deck that had been his home since awakening on the *Mayflower*.

He could see the effects of the sicknesses. Many were in their beds, and he hurried to his family's partition, his worry growing. He passed Lizzy and saw her taking care of her family, who all looked sick, too. So much sickness! He felt his body tense as he pulled his family's curtain back. There, he found both his aunt and uncle lying in bed asleep. Blake didn't want to wake them, but Aunt Ann opened her eyes.

"Henry! It is so good to see you." Her voice sounded very weak. "I didn't let them tell you we were both sick. I knew you would come, and it was more important to get the buildings finished so we could come over as soon as possible. Lizzy's family is very sick, too, so Mary Brewster is caring for Humility. Make sure you stop and see her before you go back to the colony."

"I wish I would have known you were sick," Blake said, kneeling down by her side. "We've been working hard to complete the building so everyone can leave the *Mayflower* soon. This week we will be back to take everyone home. Who is taking care of you? "

"Dr. Fuller comes as often as he can, and the healthy ones are bringing us food. I'm worried about your uncle. He really hasn't gotten his health back since that expedition. I think when we can get to our new home, we will both improve."

Blake reached down and held her small hand in his. "I can't stay now, but I'll be back to get you both."

"Godspeed, Henry. Always remember, no matter what happens, trust in Him."

Blake reached over and gave her a gentle hug. "I'll be back to get you. Don't forget that." He stood and left. His whole body was aching as he headed to find Humility. The Brewsters' partition was toward the back of the ship, so he made his way there, seeing even more sick people being cared for. He tapped on the wooden beam that held the blanket covering their area.

"Mrs. Brewster, it's Henry Samson. I'm here to see Humility." He heard movement behind the makeshift curtain, and Mary Brewster appeared holding Humility.

"Henry, it is so good to see you," she said. "And I can see that Humility is very happy to see you!" It was true. Humility leaned forward with her arms out to him and laughed out loud. He took her and held her tightly in his arms.

"She is such a good baby, but I can tell she is missing Ann," Mrs. Brewster told him. "It was just a few days ago that she became too ill to care for her. My husband William and I are glad we could take her in. Our house is completed, and we are going today to make our home there. We'll keep Humility with us until your family is safe and well. Please visit us often."

"Thank you so much. I can't stay, but I wanted to see Humility before I went back." He gave Humility a big hug and handed her back to Mrs. Brewster, bidding her goodbye as he turned and hurried out of the area. Humility started to cry as he walked away. It broke his heart to leave her.

As Blake and John were being ferried back to the shore, John spoke quietly. "It will be good, Henry, when we make the final trip and all our people are taken safely to their new home in Plymouth Colony. Life has been hard, but it will get better when we are all together. A new start in a new land."

Blake nodded but didn't reply. His thoughts were back on the *Mayflower* with his family. He was glad that Humility would be coming to live with the Brewsters in their new house today. He would stop and see her when he was able, but it was hard leaving and knowing that Aunt Ann and Uncle Edward were still on the ship. He would come and get them as soon as possible, but would it be soon enough?

These thoughts tugged at his heart.

CHAPTER FOURTEEN
WELCOME, ENGLISHMEN

Miles Standish, along with other leaders and colonists, was standing on the hilltop that overlooked Plymouth Bay when Blake and John returned from the *Mayflower*.

"This being Friday, March 16, 1621, it is our determination to elect Miles Standish as our colony's military commander." Governor Carver, still weak from his illness, stood tall as he spoke of the outstanding abilities and courage of Miles Standish. "Part of his responsibilities will be to strengthen the hilltop fortification by mounting artillery pieces in the battery."

As Blake observed the ceremony and listened to Carver speak, he looked down the street and was shocked to see a lone man approaching from the woods. He was clad only in breechcloth and was carrying a bow and two arrows in his hand. As others spotted the man and alerted everyone else, they started to scramble for weapons in alarm. The man walked boldly up the dirt street between the cottages and stood face to face with the leaders. Everyone was dumb-founded. It happened so fast that Blake barely had time to react. He felt the knife that John had given him hanging on the casing around his waist, but it was too late to draw it.

"Welcome, Englishmen!" he said. "Welcome, Englishmen!" he repeated.

He was tall and stately, and carried himself with pride and dignity. Blake knew the leaders had tried to meet peaceably with the local Native Americans, but could never find them. They only saw their fires and heard their cries in the night. And now one stood at the top of the hill staring into their eyes and speaking English! *This sounds as believable as touching a coin, being plummeted back in time, and waking up on the Mayflower.*

"My name is Samoset, and I am a leader of the Abenaki people," the man continued. "I live north of here. It is one day's sail with great wind, or five days by land. We have many providences and my people are many and strong. I learned your tongue from white men who came looking for cod fish that live in the great sea near my home. Captain Thomas Dermer dropped me off in this region in your English year 1619. I presently live as guest of the Pokanoket."

He had long black hair and was mostly naked except for a span of leather around his waist. In his hand, he carried two arrows. One had a flint arrowhead, the other had the arrowhead removed. "These arrows symbolize what we have to offer you: either war or peace." As he stood there, a cold wind started to rise, and Governor Carver placed a warm coat on his shoulders.

"Do you English have beer?" the man asked, directing his request to Governor Carver.

"No, we have aqua vitae. John and Henry, get our guest some drink and refreshment!" Governor Carver looked over at them and nodded his head.

Immediately they left and headed to the house where the food was stored. It didn't take them long to return with the drink, some biscuit, butter, cheese, pudding, and a large piece of mallard. Samoset was sitting cross-legged by the fire as John and Henry placed the tray of food before him. He nodded his approval and started to talk as he ate.

"This earth where I now sit was called Patuxet, or Little Bay. Four years ago, a terrible plague sickened all who lived here, and they died. The Pokanoket, who welcome me as a guest, and other allied tribes are ruled by a great leader named Massasoit. Along with me, another Indian speaks the language of the English. He is named Tisquantum, but the English call him Squanto."

When evening came, Governor Carver stood and asked him if it was time for him to return to the Pokanoket.

"It is my wish to spend the night here," Samoset said.

The Governor knew there was no available space for him to sleep in the colony, so he suggested, "Great Samoset, would you like to sleep on the great ship, the *Mayflower*?"

He agreed, so the group headed to the bay where the shallop was waiting on shore. He climbed aboard, but the wind was high, and the tide was low, so they had to turn back to shore. One of the members, Stephen Hopkins, who knew the general lifestyle of American Indians from previous explorations in America, stepped forward.

"Governor Carver, I would be honored for the Great Samoset to lodge in my house tonight." And so, it was agreed.

In the morning, Blake watched as three gifts were given to Samoset: a knife, a bracelet, and a ring. Samoset accepted them, saying, "I will return with some of our neighbors. They will have beaver skins to trade." With that said, he left and headed back through the woods.

There was still much to do at Plymouth Colony. Blake and John went to work side by side, placing mortar in the cracks of a cottage to seal off the wind and cold.

"Henry, I think that was the greatest surprise I ever had in my whole life!" John exclaimed. "I couldn't believe my eyes as I saw Samoset walking boldly up our street! I didn't know if we should run for cover or stand our ground, but there was no time to do anything. We have tried so many times to meet our neighbors with no success....and here he comes walking up the middle of the street calling out, 'Welcome, Englishmen!'"

Blake could see the whole scene play again in his head. "I know. I am still amazed. And he came to offer war or peace. Did you see the two arrows? Perhaps we will share their land as friends." His thoughts turned to the ship and those still remaining aboard. "And

Captain Jones must prepare for his voyage back to England. There are many sick on the *Mayflower* and here in the common house, too. I don't see how we can make room for more, but I will feel better to have Uncle Edward and Aunt Ann here to help care for them."

"Well, spring is almost here, and the weather continues to clear." John sounded hopeful. "Having all our people together here will be much safer. Master Carver said there were eight deaths in January and 17 more deaths in February. It has been very hard to bury them on the hillside at night to keep the number of deaths a secret from the Indians. It will be good to have everyone here together!"

March 21, 1621: The day had finally arrived to get the rest of the Pilgrims from the *Mayflower*. Blake and John stood on the hillside looking out over the bay to the site where the ship sat. The weather was cold with a light breeze, but the sun was shining. It would be good to bring everyone home. The shallop shuttled the men through the bay. Blake was the first to climb the ladder and find his way down the ladder to his family below. There was much activity as people packed up their meager belongings in anticipation of this final trip. He passed the partition where Mr. Chilton used to sit and call out greetings to him. It was quiet and bare. He had died in December while they were still in Cape Cod Harbor, and his wife died in early winter. Mary, his daughter, was one of the girls caring for the sick at the common house. Blake continued forward in the dim light, remembering Mr. Chilton fondly.

"Hi, Henry!" It was Lizzy Tilley. She was packing up the things around Aunt Ann and Uncle Edward. "I got everything ready in my family's area, and now I'm helping prepare your partition. We are all happy to get to the colony. Maybe the sickness will get better when we are off the *Mayflower*."

"Thanks, Lizzy! There are many sick there, too. But it will be good to have everyone home." He saw Aunt Ann sitting up on her bed, but she looked pale and weak. Uncle Edward did not even stir. They would need extra care and aid to get them aboard the shallop. He could hear John making his way over, calling out greetings as always.

"Hi, Lizzy," John greeted her. "I'm here to help get your family and belongings to the deck." They looked at each other and Lizzy's cheeks turned bright pink.

"Thanks, John, but there are many here who need help, too."

"Yes, I'll get your family first, and then I will come back for the sicker ones." John turned to Blake. "Henry, I will get Mistress Ann and Master Edward when I return. We are getting the healthy ones first, so we can take extra care with the sick."

They worked together to get everyone to the deck above, carrying the sick and placing them in the sun. Each waited their turn as the shallop returned to carry more ashore. Blake helped as much as he could with everyone. They were down to the final trip now, and Blake went to Aunt Ann.

"We're ready to take you and Uncle Edward next. You are the last passengers to leave the *Mayflower*."

She looked up and smiled. "The sun feels so good on my face. I am happy to be going ashore. It will be good to be in a house on dry land. Her eyes seemed an even brighter blue than usual as they filled with tears.

"You are going to stay in the common house so we can take care of you," Blake assured her. "It will be good to have you home." He squeezed her hand as John came over to help get them aboard the shallop with the last passengers. "It's time to go now."

It was very difficult moving Uncle Edward. They wrapped him tightly and lowered him to the boat. They both looked back as the *Mayflower* moored quietly in Plymouth Bay, its final passengers released to the New World. Soon, she would be heading back to England.

There were many on shore to help carry the last passengers up the hill. Plymouth Colony was finally, and officially, their new home.

The sickness seemed inescapable. Blake thought it would get easier having his aunt and uncle in the common house, but it got worse. Some days, two or three of those who were sick died. The women tended the sick at first, but soon they became ill, too. He would see Lizzy and other women up early cooking in the huge iron pots, but the sick barely ate. Blake would try to get Aunt Ann and Uncle Edward to eat a little of the thin broth from the stew, but they could eat nothing. Uncle Edward mumbled and talked randomly about people and things that made no sense.

The next day, Blake was in the woods all day cutting and splitting wood for the colony. It was getting dark as he approached the common house with the last armful of wood, and he noticed Captain Standish standing outside the entrance. It had been a long day, and Blake was exhausted. His arms ached from carrying the wood, and he was anxious to check on Uncle Edward and Aunt Ann. The closer he got, the more worried he became. Why was Standish just standing there? As he stacked the wood in the woodpile, Standish came over to him.

"Henry, I need to speak with you." Standish stood there and put his hand on Blake's shoulder.

"Henry, it pains me to tell you that both your aunt and uncle passed away today while you were in the woods. They were always so close; I'm not surprised they died within hours of each other. With all the sickness, we were not able to send anyone to get you. Several of the men, including John, are at the hill digging the graves. We carefully wrapped them and are on our way now with their bodies."

Blake was shocked. "How can that be? I thought they would get better once they were here with us!"

Standish patted his shoulder and offered his sympathy for his loss before directing him to follow the wooden rack carrying the bodies to their final resting place.

It was dark when Blake and those carrying the wooden rack

reached the grave site. He felt numb all over. John was waiting for him to arrive and came to him, placing his arm around his shoulder.

"Henry, I am sorry," he murmured. "They were very kind and loving people, and they will be sorely missed. It was obvious they both loved you and Humility very much." Blake couldn't even speak. He just nodded. They all knelt at the open hole as the bodies were lowered into the fresh earth.

Reverend William Brewster called out in the darkness, "We thank you, oh God, for the lives of Ann and Edward Tilley. We know you called them unto yourself. We pray for Henry and Humility as they continue in this new land. Lord, we pray for your peace and continued grace upon our lives. Ashes to ashes, dust to dust. Amen."

With that, they covered the bodies with the fresh dirt and then headed up the hill. The stars were brilliant in the sky and the moon helped guide their steps. He felt the coin rub against his leg in his pocket.

What will I do now? This seems too real for a dream. Is there a way home, a way back? I will make sure baby Humility is taken care of. Surely there is a way home. Right? As he closed his eyes for a moment, he saw the loving face of Aunt Ann and heard her voice. *"Godspeed, Henry."*

Once they returned, Blake sat outside the common house alone, wrapped in a blanket. He could not share this pain with anyone. The floodgates opened and he was pelted with emotions he had never experienced before. His heart was in the midst of a heavy gale, and he was being violently tossed about. Could he weather the storms in this cold and unpredictable land...alone?

Godspeed, Aunt Ann. I will never forget you and Uncle Edward.

———————

The illness continued to plague the colony. Soon almost everyone was sick in bed. Blake and John were among seven people who worked tirelessly taking care of the them. Sometimes, when he would change the beds and carry the loathsome bedding out to the washing tub, he would run to the side of the hill and throw up. *I will not give up!* Blake repeated this over and over to himself. *I need to do all I can to help.* Reverend Brewster and Captain Standish were among those who cheerfully and willingly did whatever was necessary, too.

Lizzy Tilley lost both her mother and father to the sickness. She was all alone now. Still, she continued working hard and caring for all who needed her. Many times, she would get Humility and bring her over to see Blake.

"She helps me ease the pain of losing my parents," said Lizzy as she chased the cute toddler around. I have no other family here, but you and Humility. I pray that soon the sickness will end.

CHAPTER FIFTEEN

A PROMISE OF PEACE

True to his word, Samoset returned to the colony a few days later and brought with him five Pokanoket men. John came to find Blake to tell him the news: "Henry, Samoset has returned with some of his people!"

Blake put down the axe he had been using to split firewood and followed John to the center of town. It was thrilling to see the strange-looking men. They each had deerskin leggings and a leather loin-cloth that hung down from their waists. Their long, dark hair was adorned with feathers, and one tall man also had a fox tail hanging out of his hair. Blake nudged John to get his attention. "Look, one even has a wildcat's skin on his arm. They have no weapons."

"I heard Miles Standish tell Samoset he needed to leave bows and arrows outside of town when he returned," John explained. "It is a sign of peace and trust."

"Thank you for returning and bringing your friends, Samoset,"

Governor Carver said, capturing the boys' attention. "We are honored that you are here. Let us celebrate." He motioned for the guests to sit. One of the men got out his fiddle and started to play lively music while others brought out food to share. After a time, the Pokanoket in their turn started to sing and dance as was their custom. It was entertaining for everyone, especially after all the death and sickness.

After the festivities, Samoset stood and addressed everyone. "I am Samoset, and this is my friend, Tisquantum," he said, motioning to one of the native men. "You English call him Squanto. He speaks your tongue very well." He nodded to Squanto.

Squanto then said, "I am a friend of the English and would like to help you speak to Massasoit, the great king of many tribes and people. We will tell him of the respect and peace you have made known to us today. If it is his desire to meet you, we will return." With that, Squanto and the other Pokanoket men stood and walked down the dirt road and into the woods.

When they were gone, Governor Carver spoke to all. "This was a very important meeting. After the many times we've tried to contact the people who live here, God has prepared a way for our people to meet and possibly to live in peace. By the grace of God, we will be waiting to see when the next meeting will be."

The meeting came sooner than anyone expected. Many of the men were still working to finish the cottages, and Blake was bundling thatch for a roof. It was a fair, warm day, and the men were glad to be outdoors.

Samoset, Squanto, and three others arrived without warning; upon seeing them, Captain Standish moved to meet them in the center of the town. Governor Carver joined the group.

Squanto stepped forward and spoke, "The Great Chief Massasoit and his brother, Quadequina, want to meet with the governor up on the hill."

They looked up the hill and there stood at least 60 men looking down at them. Their faces were painted many colors. Some had skins on, while others looked almost naked. They all looked well-armed. It was a very formidable-looking gathering.

"Squanto, tell your great king that we cannot send our governor to him. They must come here to our wigwam." Captain Standish spoke with great authority.

The Indians left again and headed to the top of the hill. They talked among themselves, and after a time, Squanto and the group returned and replied, "Our Great Chief Massasoit has sent word that he cannot come here. You must come to him."

Blake anxiously watched as the leaders talked together and again stepped back to Squanto. This time, it was Governor Carver who spoke.

"We will send another one of our great leaders, Edward Winslow, to talk with Chief Massasoit." The Governor motioned to Edward Winslow and he stepped forward. "I am the governor, and this honorable leader knows and can speak of my will to have peace and trading between our great nations. Now, please allow us to prepare gifts for your great king, Chief Massasoit, and his brother, Quadequina."

There was a scurry of activity as orders were given to gather the food and gifts for Massasoit and his brother.

"John Howland and Henry Samson will accompany you," Governor Carver continued. John and Blake stepped forward and acknowledged Squanto with respect. The food and gifts were packed in a small wooden cart and the entourage moved slowly to the hilltop. Chief Massasoit and his brother, Quadequina, slid down off their ponies as the group approached.

"Great Chief Massasoit, please accept these gifts as a token of our gratitude and friendship." As Edward Winslow spoke, he handed the chief each gift. First was a pair of knives. "These knives are forged of the finest material and the handles are carved of silver." The Chief took the knives and carefully examined them. He nodded his approval.

Each time he spoke, William Winslow waited as Squanto translated his words into their native language.

Winslow continued, "Please also accept this fine copper chain adorned with a beautiful English jewel. See how the sun dances in its heart." Chief Massasoit held the necklace and moved it back and forth to see it glitter in the sun. Again, he nodded his approval and placed the chain and pendant around his neck. It rested on his bare chest against a huge bear claw and many strings of colorful beads.

Winslow turned and faced Quadequina. "And for the brother of the Great Chief Massasoit, fine knives made in our great country that stretches across the sea, and a beautiful jewel to adorn the ear of Quadequina." He slowly examined each piece and nodded his approval. His hand went quickly to his ear as he replaced the current earring with the new gift. It sparkled in the sunlight as it dangled from his ear.

"We also bring a pot of aqua vitae, biscuits, and butter." John and Blake carried the food and placed it at their feet.

"Please sit, eat, and drink as we celebrate your presence here," said Edward Winslow. Chief Massasoit, Quadequina, Squanto, and Edward Winslow all sat together in a circle.

Winslow continued talking as they sat and started to eat and drink together. "Our King James, who lives on the other side of the great ocean, salutes you with his words of love and peace, and wants you as his friend. Also, our Governor Carver desires to see you and trade with you and confirm peace with you as a great neighbor." Edward Winslow expressed himself well as he conveyed the greetings.

The four men sat there and enjoyed their meal together. No one seemed in a hurry as the biscuits and butter were passed around, and the last of the strong water was sipped. When they were finished, Chief Massasoit was the first to rise, and the others followed.

After speaking back and forth with Chief Massasoit, Squanto stepped forward to Edward Winslow. "Our great chief likes your speech and would like to meet your chiefs at the brook and speak as brothers."

"I will go and tell the leaders of this great honor." Winslow and the convoy bowed low and headed back down the hill. Blake's heart was racing so fast, he feared he might fall and tumble down the hill.

Upon returning to Plymouth Colony, Edward Winslow relayed Chief Massasoit's wishes to the leaders.

Captain Standish spoke first. "I will go to the brook and meet the chief and his party there. I will take a dozen men with muskets with us. Because they have already seen them both, I will also take John Howland and Henry Samson as well."

Blake could barely control his excitement. This was more than he had ever imagined. *I just pinched myself hard…and it hurt! I can't be dreaming this. I don't think anyone feels a pinch in a dream. Right?*

Blake and John followed Captain Standish and his dozen men down to the brook. When they reached the bank, the Pokanoket were all on the other side. It was an amazing sight to see. Both sides lined up and faced each other.

Captain Standish walked across the brook, stood at attention, and saluted Chef Massasoit. He then returned.

Chief Massasoit slid off his pony, walked across the brook, and saluted Captain Standish. When he returned to his side of the brook, Squanto walked over and spoke. "Chief Massasoit wishes to go to your wigwam."

Blake gave a big sigh of relief. This seemed to be a ceremony of honor and respect. There was no fighting or harsh words or disrespect in any way. *I wonder if I will read about this in my history book. Will anyone believe I was here at the brook, watching this great tribute and alliance of peace? Do I believe I am here?*

Captain Standish turned and said, "John and Henry, run back and tell Governor Carver that Chief Massasoit is coming back to the colony!"

They were breathless when they found Governor Carver outside the common house.

John spoke, "Master Carver, the Chief is coming back here. They did a big ceremony at the brook, and they are coming now." He had just finished talking when the procession could be seen returning from the brook.

"Thanks, John." Governor Carver was smiling.

Captain Standish led the way up the dirt road, and the Pokanoket guests followed. The small community watched in wonder as Captain Standish stepped inside one of the unfinished cottages.

He looked at Blake. "Find a chair, rug, and four cushions, and bring them back here!" Blake left immediately and found Mistress Carver standing by the road.

"Mistress Carver, Captain Standish needs a chair, a rug, and four cushions. They are having a meeting with the Pokanoket chief in the unfinished hut." She went to her small house and gathered up the requested items, handing them to Blake who carried them back to Captain Standish. He placed the green rug on the dirt floor, and cushion on the chair.

Chief Massasoit, his brother, and Squanto entered the unfinished cottage. Instantly, Governor Carver came in with one man playing a drum and another blowing a trumpet behind him.

"Welcome, great and mighty Massasoit!" Carver took his hand and kissed it. The king returned the kiss. "Please sit down. Just as our King James who rules from across the great ocean sits on a great throne, we give you the seat of honor in our presence." Directing his voice to the colonists, Carver said, "Bring us some strong water so we may drink to each other!" Outside, someone ran to get tankards full of the brew.

Once they arrived, Carver said, "To the mighty King Massasoit and to the Governor of this Plymouth Colony. May we make peace with each other for the good of our two mighty nations." They raised their cups, drank, and were seated. Carver also asked for fresh roasted meat to be served to the Chief and Quadequina.

When they were finished eating and drinking, they started the process of making peace. Carver looked to John and said, "John Howland, get your paper and quill. We have much to write down."

John left and returned quickly with the required items.

As each leader talked and discussed the fair and equal treatment of both nations, Squanto would interpret their words for the others. When something was agreed upon, John would write it down. When they were all finished, John read the agreement exactly as it was stated. The agreement was as follows:

1. *That neither he nor any of his should injure or do hurt to any of our people.*

2. *And if any of his did hurt to any of ours, he should send the offender, that we might punish him.*

3. *That if any of our tools were taken away when our people are at work, he should cause them to be restored, and if ours did any harm to any of his, we would do likewise to them.*

4. *If any did unjustly war against him, we would aid him; if any did war against us, he should aid us.*

5. *He should send to his neighbor confederates, to certify them of this, that they might not wrong us, but might be likewise comprised in the conditions of peace.*

6. *That when their men came to us, they should leave their bows and arrows behind them, as we should do our pieces when we came to them.*

7. *Lastly, that doing this, King James would esteem of him as his friend and ally.*

After John read the document to all who attended, it was applauded by everyone. Peace! A promise of peace between two mighty nations.

When they were finished, Governor Carver walked back to the brook with Massasoit. They embraced each other, and each departed to his own home.

A prayer of thanksgiving was on his lips as Governor Carver walked the quiet dusty road back to the friends and family of Plymouth Colony. There was the promise of peace between nations, and the promise of peace that comes only from Almighty God.

The Saturday following the great meeting with Massasoit, Edward Winslow's wife died of the illness, taking the rising death toll in March to 13, and the total deaths to 45. Would winter ever end, or the sting of death from illness stop? If not, soon there would be no one left at the Plymouth Colony, just like the Patuxet, who lived there before them.

CHAPTER SIXTEEN

SPRING AT LAST

When April finally arrived, seven houses had been completed at Plymouth Colony. On April 5, 1621, everyone gathered on the hilltop to watch the *Mayflower* turn seaward and head back to England. Of the 30 original seamen, only 13 lived to make this return trip. When given the choice, John Alden, who had originally been hired for a year as ship's crewman to maintain the ship's barrels, had agreed to stay, too. He saw great promise in this new land and wanted the opportunity to build a new life here.

Despite all the hardships and death, every passenger who survived the long winter decided to remain at their new home in America. Blake stood by himself and watched until the *Mayflower* was completely out of sight. *I will save this picture in my memory forever - the beauty of the calm sea as the Mayflower slowly disappeared on the horizon.*

As Blake finally turned away, Squanto walked from the woods

and up the road, and approached Governor Carver.

"My friends of the Plymouth Colony, there is much work to do. The Pokanoket have freed me to be a guide between our mighty nations. I speak the tongue of the English and the Pokanoket. I will live with you and teach you many good and necessary things, and I will be a brother to the English."

Governor Carver came and grabbed his hand. "Let me shake the hand of my brother Squanto," he said fervently. "You can live in the cottage with Edward Winslow and Henry Samson. Henry's relatives recently died, and Edward's wife died right after the great peace treaty between our nations. If you follow me, I will lead you to your new home."

Governor Carver and Squanto walked up the dirt road to the Winslow home. The governor saw Henry ahead, standing by the cottage, stacking wood in the woodpile.

"Here is where you can stay," indicated Governor Carver.

"Henry, Squanto is going to live with you and Edward. Please help him get settled. We will talk later; I will find Edward and tell him the news."

Blake could not believe what he was hearing. I am staying in the house with Squanto! When he was in American History class, there were two names he remembered: John Howland and Squanto, and he was lucky enough to get to know them both!

"Squanto, my name is Blake...I mean...I am...I am...Henry

Samson, and I hope to be your friend." Blake started to stammer when he said his real name out loud. *Blake....my name is Blake.* It was the first time he had said his name out loud since he talked to Humility on the *Mayflower. My real name sounded so strange to me.*

Squanto looked at Blake with his dark brown eyes and nodded a greeting. His long hair was braided, and three large bird feathers were secured in the back. His leather pants reminded Blake of the chaps that cowboys wore at rodeos. His long boots were made of the same leather, with a long fringe. The fur on his shoulder looked like it was made of bear, and around his neck was a necklace with many bear claws and beautiful blue beads. He was lean, very muscular, and stood tall and proud.

"I know you from my many walks here. You are always with another Englishman who looks older than you, like a brother. You both were there the day of the Great Peace Treaty with the Mighty Chief Massasoit. Your brother wrote down the words of peace between our two nations. We now are brothers." He reached behind his head and pulled out one of feathers. "I give this to my young brother, Henry Samson. It is from the great eagle, the strongest and bravest of all birds, and the Creator. This symbolizes trust...honor... strength... wisdom...power...and freedom." Squanto said each word separately and with conviction. "When I was walking here, this feather fell unexpectedly from the sky and I know now its purpose was to place honor upon my brother Henry Samson. Feathers may arrive unexpectedly, but not without purpose."

Blake stood unable to speak for a moment. When his words returned, he said, "Sir, I have done nothing to earn such an honor. There are many here that deserve this more than I do. Are you sure you don't want to keep it? Or give it to someone else? John Howland is braver and wiser than I am. He should have it! He is a wonderful, brave friend...he deserves it, not me."

Squanto shook his head. "My brave brother, Henry Samson, I feel the wind has whispered in my ear that you are the owner the feather was searching for. This great feather of the eagle was intended for you. You must accept it and be thankful you were chosen for this high honor. Now you must live up to its powerful symbols."

Blake looked into the wise eyes of Squanto. He reached out and accepted the feather and his new friend. "I thank you, my new brother, and I accept the challenge the feather bestows."

As they stood together, Squanto reached out, grabbed a handful of Blake's curly hair, and started to braid a long strand. It had grown shoulder-length since his unexpected arrival on the *Mayflower*. Taking the eagle feather from Blake's hand, Squanto skillfully wove its end into Blake's hair. It hung right beside his ear.

"You are now a young brave and a brother to the Pokanoket," Squanto declared. "Let us go out to the hillside that overlooks the Great Bay. Go and find your brother, John Howland, and meet me there. I will tell you of my long journey to return here to Patuxet, or Plymouth, as is the new English name."

Blake hurried to find John, the feather secured in his hair. He

knocked at the door of the Carver house, and Mrs. Carver opened the door. "Are you looking for John? I sent him to get more firewood. You'll probably find Lizzy Tilley with him, wherever he is," she said with a knowing smile.

Sure enough, Blake found John chopping wood with Lizzy close by stirring what looked like peas and some kind of stew in the big iron pot. It smelled good.

"Hi, Lizzy! It's a beautiful day to be outside," Blake greeted her. "I think spring is really here, at last." She waved to him in return.

Turning to John, Blake said, "John, Squanto came and told Governor Carver that he is going to live here at Plymouth Colony. He will be staying with me at Edward Winslow's house. Can you come with me to the hill overlooking the bay? He wants to talk to us."

"Is that a feather hanging in your hair? Where did you get it?" John was quizzing him.

"Squanto found it and gave it to me. It is an eagle feather. I will tell you about it later." Blake wasn't ready to tell John the whole story about the feather yet.

John shrugged. "I'm just finishing chopping this wood for Mrs. Carver. Help me carry it to our house, and I will go with you."

Together they carried and stacked the wood outside the Carver house, then walked to the hill where Squanto sat looking out at the bay.

When they both arrived, Squanto nodded and pointed to an area for them to sit.

"John Howland, you have been important in the journey to peace and understanding with my people. You and Henry are my brothers." Squanto touched a small beaded necklace that hung around his neck. It had two bear claws attached. He pulled it over his head and placed it around John's neck. "This will be a sign of our brotherhood. The bear represents a protector. It symbolizes courage, physical strength, and leadership. Bears are strong, agile, and quick, just as you have been, John Howland. You will be a strong leader to your people and serve them well."

"Thank you, Squanto," John said humbly. "This is a great honor. I truly feel like your brother. When I left England, my brothers stayed behind, hoping to join me one day here. Henry helped to save my life when I was swept overboard in a fierce storm. He also became my brother. Now—I have many brothers."

As they sat there, Squanto started to speak again. "I want to tell you, my brothers, the strange story of my long journey from my home here, and back again. I was born here in the year you call 1590. My people were called the Patuxet. They were the ones who cleared this land, planted corn, and fished and hunted here. I sat on this very hill and looked out over this bay before I was stolen away from my people. My father was an important chief and leader, and I was raised to lead, too. White men came many times to our land and fished and traded with my people. Captain John Smith came with a man called Thomas Dermer. They were good and honorable men.

We traded furs with them. They knew we were a people of honor.

"When Smith left, a new ship came to the bay. This captain's name was Thomas Hunt and he said he was a friend of Smith's. He wanted us to come to his ship and talk about great trade. But Hunt was no friend. When 20 of us were aboard, he confined us below deck and sailed across Cape Cod Bay. There he stole seven more from the Nauset tribe and then set sail for Malaga in the faraway country of Spain. It was a long journey, but I am a 'pniese,' a man of courage. I stayed strong and urged my people to stay strong.

"Hunt had intended to sell us as slaves, but there were men who served the Creator who set us free. They were called friars, or brothers. They taught me the language of the English and spoke to me of the Christian faith. I lived four years among them. One day, they came to me and put me on a ship to England. 'Go back to your people, to your home,' they told me. 'You have learned much and will be a great leader for your people.'

"After leaving Spain, I lived in Cornhill in the city of London with Master John Slanie. He is a merchant and shipbuilder. I was there two years, finally sailing back across the great sea to a land north of here called Newfoundland. There I heard reports of the terrible plague that killed many up and down the coast. I was anxious to get back to Cape Cod Bay and find my family. When I came here, the sickness had taken all but two of this village, and now I am the only one left. My whole family, my wife, my children, my parents— all had been taken. I cannot say their names until I also climb the highest mountain and walk the road to the Creator of All Things."

"I am sorry for your great loss, Squanto. I also have lost my family," Blake said. Tears stung his eyes as he thought about Uncle Edward and Aunt Ann. *Will I ever see Mom and Dad, Jackson, Layla, and Annie again?*

Squanto shook his head and looked out to sea. "Then truly we are brothers and family to each other."

He continued his story. "The people here were very angry at the white people who had lied and stolen us to sell as slaves. That is why they would not meet with your leaders here when you tried to find them. They did not trust you. Much has happened here. Where there were once thousands, now there are only hundreds.

"I wanted to bring peace to our two nations. I talked to the great Chief Massasoit about becoming friends. So, he watched your people this winter, and finally agreed to talk peace with you. There was still much deep pain remaining from those families that had been kidnapped. I saw a woman on one of my meetings. She looked to be about 100 years old. She told us Hunt had taken her three sons and now she was deprived of the comfort of her children in her old age. She could not even look at us without weeping and crying. I am here now to help carry out the peace and teach you to plant crops, to hunt for food, and to fish the Great Bay. We will be brothers in this great plan."

The three sat there and stared out at the vast ocean. The sun would soon be setting.

"Tomorrow, I will begin teaching you and your people," Squanto said. "It will be the start of a great day!"

That night, after dinner in the common house, they went back to Edward Winslow's house, rolled out their mats, and slept. Blake kept the eagle feather tied in his hair and the coin tucked away in his pocket. It had been a good day.

———————

Squanto was a man of his word. The next morning, bright and early, he was in the fields. All able-bodied men, women, and children came to help. "First, we must burn the fields to clear away the undergrowth," he told them. "This will make for a better harvest in the fall." So, they set fire to the field and tended it, so the fire did not get carried away. Everyone smelled like smoke when they came in from the fields that day.

The next day, Squanto led them to a place called Eel River. They carried several buckets with them. When he got to the muddy banks, Squanto kicked the buried eels out of the mud. Blake found it amazing and fun to watch. He shouted to Squanto, "My brother, you capture food with your bow and arrow and your toes!" Everyone laughed.

That night, they ate eels that were fat and sweet. *I have never eaten an eel before, but they were good.* After being hungry for so many months, with very little food to eat, Blake wasn't as picky as he used to be. He now appreciated the food that was set before him.

The word had traveled quickly that Squanto would be teaching the colonists how to plant seeds, and that many hands were necessary. Anyone who wanted to eat had to work. They removed many heavy rocks from the soil, and it was back-breaking work. At lunch, Blake went to the brook to soak his aching, blistered hands in the cold water. He thought of his mom and sisters who loved to work in the garden at home. *I will remember to thank them for all their hard work when I get home. No, IF I get home again.* He felt an instant stab of homesickness.

When he returned to the field, Squanto had directed everyone to gather buckets and start walking toward the bay. "Why are we going to the shore?" Blake asked curiously. "I thought we were planting seeds today."

Squanto looked at Blake and replied, "Be patient, little brother. I have much to teach you today. See the small fish that have washed up on the shore? We will need as many as you can find." Soon, the buckets were overflowing. Occasionally, fish spilled out on the ground as the colonists walked back up the hill to the open field.

"Bury these fish with the seeds of the three sisters: the corn, beans, and squash. They will grow and give you plenty." Squanto instructed them to make mounds with the soil using their hands or seashells for tools. "When the corn sprouts, you will add bean seeds to the same mounds. The corn stalks help support the bean runners. The squash vines will be trained along the mounds to protect the corn stalk roots and reduce weeds. That is why we call them the three sisters. This was the work of the women from our village. My work was and is to hunt and fish."

After the fields were planted, Squanto also took them into the woods to look for game. They set many traps to catch deer and hunted the ducks that were abundant in the surrounding lakes.

Because they had no family to spend their spare time with, John, Blake, and Squanto became like true blood brothers. They were now family. It was common for them to hang out together and talk by themselves.

"John, remember our first expedition to get firewood when we picked the juniper branches that were on the ground? My arms ached from carrying them to the shallop and then to the *Mayflower*. I fell asleep that night to the smell of burning juniper. Aunt Ann was so happy to have fragrant wood to burn." Blake closed his eyes for a moment. He could smell the juniper and still see her holding Humility and cooking supper.

John smiled. "Yes, Henry, and here we are in the woods again. I'm thankful the bitter cold is gone."

"My brothers, that was the first time you landed in the Freezing Moon of 1620," Squanto said. "I stood with the Pokanoket, hidden in the woods as you gathered the wood. Massasoit watched silently that first winter. We were very interested to see what your intentions were. Many moons we observed you without your knowledge."

John spoke up, saying, "We wanted to meet you, but we could never find you. Our men heard your cries in the night and saw your fires."

"Massasoit did not trust the white men. He waited and watched. But now we have peace between our nations. Now we are brothers."

They all agreed and quietly marveled at the bond that existed between them.

Spring was finally becoming apparent. The days were longer and warmer. It was about a month after the *Mayflower* sailed back to England that Governor Carver was working in the fields when suddenly he fell to his knees, complaining of a pain in his head. The men carried him back to his house.

Soon after, Governor Carver fell into a coma. Even though Mrs. Carver worked around the clock caring for her sick husband, he did not recover, and died at the end of three days. All of Plymouth Colony lamented his death. After all the secret burials that were performed all winter, the settlers wished to bury the governor with as much ceremony as possible. The whole town walked to the hillside where so many of their friends and family had been buried. The Pilgrims understood that the life which awaited them in America included dangers and challenges aplenty, but this was a big blow to everyone. Mrs. Carver was inconsolable.

William Bradford was voted in as the new governor of Plymouth

Colony. He spoke with great passion at the grave site, saying, "Despite all our fears, we have chosen to go forward in this land. I believe that all great and honorable actions are accompanied by great difficulties and must be both met and overcome with answerable courage. We commend to God a great yet humble man who answered the call with the greatest courage. He is no longer a sojourner here on this earth. Almighty God has called him home and now gives rest in His peace. Amen."

Captain Standish had his men stand at attention, and as they placed the last shovel full of earth on the mound, they fired off a volley of shots in his honor. Because of the peace the late Governor Carver had helped secure, they no longer had to bury their loved ones in the dark. The mourners turned and quietly walked up the dusty road to their homes at the top of the hill.

A few weeks later, they would make the trek to the hillside to bury Mistress Carver. Blake believed what many said to be true— Katherine Carver died of a broken heart.

After the death of John and Katherine Carver, John Howland was saddened, but was touched by the generosity and thoughtfulness of his *Mayflower* family. He would miss them greatly.

"I received a small inheritance and will continue to live in the Carver's cottage. It is now my home," John told Blake one day. "He was a good, generous, and honorable man. I miss him. He treated me like a son and taught me so many things that will enable me to have a good life here. And Mistress Carver was kind. She nursed me back to health after I was rescued from my watery grave. I owe them both a great debt of gratitude. I am no longer an indentured servant. I am now a free man." Pausing for a moment, John looked at Blake and said, "Because you are my brothers, my family, it would be good if you and Squanto came to live with me. I would appreciate your company."

"Thank you, John. That sounds amazing! I'll see if Governor Bradford approves it."

Blake was thrilled when it was approved.

He liked his life here. He spent time with John and Squanto hunting, fishing, and looking for mussels and clams in the bay. Everything was turning green. They found white and red grapes that were very sweet. Blake ate so many, he almost got sick. There were even strawberries, gooseberries (which Blake hadn't seen or tasted before), raspberries, and plums.

In May, the colony celebrated their first wedding. It was a very simple ceremony presided over by Governor Bradford and attended by all the surviving settlers. Edward Winslow and Susanna White had both lost their spouses in the winter's great sickness. Just like the promise of spring, this happy event signaled the survival of Plymouth Colony, and served as a promise and hope for the future.

Governor Bradford sent Squanto on a mission to see Chief Massasoit and his people. He returned bearing messages of goodwill from the chief; the peace treaty was being honored and upheld. Bradford sent another team to establish a measure of peace with other tribes in the region. He also paid the Nauset's for the corn that the Pilgrims had taken during their first expedition ashore. Without it, they may have starved. As a member of that expedition, Blake felt good knowing their debt was paid.

Blake checked on Humility every day, just as he had promised his Uncle Edward. She was adjusting to her new life with the Brewsters. She still would reach her arms out for him to hold her, but was always ready to go back to Mistress Brewster. *Maybe I can go home now that my promise has been fulfilled.* He thought about going home every day now. Sometimes, he would handle the coin, but nothing ever happened. *Will I know when it's really time to go? Will this mysterious coin take me back home again?*

CHAPTER SEVENTEEN
SUMMER AND FEAST OF HARVEST - THANKSGIVING

During the summer, Blake spent most of his time with Squanto. They would search the woods for many kinds of game, and Squanto would tell Blake stories of his people.

"I think of how our two people have become intertwined. And I feel hope for our children in seasons to come. I have seen both death and life come to this land that gives itself to English and Indian alike." Squanto looked at Blake for a moment. "Henry Samson, you do not talk much of your family. You always seem to be thinking of other things."

"John and I went above the grates on the *Mayflower* during a fierce storm. A huge wave caught him and sent him overboard. When I tried to help him, I slipped, hit my head, and lost my memory. When I woke up, Aunt Ann was talking care of me. I don't remember anything that happened here before the storm."

"There is something I sense in your spirit, for I have known it myself. You have a deep longing to be somewhere else," Squanto observed. "This does not seem to be your true home."

"You are right, this does not feel like my true home," Blake admitted. "Maybe my memory will return someday, and I will find my way back to my people."

After this conversation with Squanto, the thought of going home burned ever stronger in his heart.

The days of summer were long, and the crops continued to grow. Some of the English crops had not done well, but Blake watched with joy as the three sisters—corn, beans, and squash—grew well, and the fields were heavy with great bounty.

Governor Bradford called Squanto and the Pilgrims together one fall day.

"God be praised! It seems the sicknesses have finally ended. We are now beginning to gather the harvest and fit up our houses and dwellings against winter. All 51 of our surviving people have recovered in health and strength. And thanks to our brother, Squanto, we have learned how to plant seeds, catch fish, and hunt game. Our neighbors have been very faithful in their covenant of peace with us and very loving towards us. We often go to them, and they come to us as well. And we walk as peaceably and safely in the wood as in the highways of England. We entertain them in our houses and they in turn welcome us. They are very trustworthy, quick-witted, and just.

"I never in my life remember a more seasonable summer than we have enjoyed. Many of you say it is colder in winter, but I cannot say out of my experience. The air is very clear and not foggy, as has been reported. I believe men might live here as contented as in any part of the world.

"For fish and fowl, we have great abundance; fresh cod in the summer and our bay is full of lobsters all the summer and affords a variety of other fish. In September, we can take a great bounty of eels in a night with small labor and can dig them out of their beds all the winter. We have mussels at our doors. Oysters we have none near, but we can have them brought by our good neighbors, the Pokanoket, when we will; all the springtime the earth sends forth naturally very good salad greens. Here are grapes, white and red, and very sweet and strong also. Strawberries, gooseberries, raspberries, and plums of three sorts. There is an abundance of roses, white, red, and damask; very sweet-smelling indeed.

"This new country needs only industrious men and women to live here. And being the truth of things, I take knowledge of, that we might now, on our behalf give God thanks who has dealt so favorably with us. It is time to have a thanksgiving observation, The Feast of Harvest, to celebrate God's grace and provision at harvest time. This will be a three-day event. Today, I will send out a four-man hunting party to obtain game for our celebrations. We will begin to plan field sports and activities. The entertainment will include wrestling, footraces, and jumping contests. Also, Captain Standish will oversee target-shooting and firing demonstrations. Because we have gathered the fruit of our labors, we will rejoice together in this special manner.

"Let the celebration begin!"

The four-man hunting party was officially dispatched and returned later in the day with a week's supply of turkeys, partridges, and quail. The four married women who had survived the first winter, along with a few servants, set to work getting the fires ready and boiling water in the iron pots. Even the children were busy washing the vegetables and getting more wood for the fires. Workers set up makeshift tables throughout the village, and benches, chairs, small barrels, and baskets for people to sit upon.

Mistress Brewster called to a few young girls nearby, "Set the table with the trenchers and pewter plates. And don't forget the knives and spoons." Blake was nearby, bringing more wood for the fires. He watched as Humility toddled around, carrying a wooden plate in her hands.

"Hello, Mistress Brewster. It is a beautiful day for a celebration," Blake said. "And what, might I ask, is a trencher? You told the girls to set the table with trenchers and pewter plates."

She smiled at him. "A trencher is a square wooden plate. Humility is supposed to be taking one to Lizzy to set the table."

Humility heard his voice and hurried over to see him. She laughed and put up her arms.

"Hello, little Miss Humility," Blake smiled. "Do you want me to pick you up?" He knelt, swooped her up in his arms and swung her around in a circle. The wooden plate escaped from her tiny grasp, and she giggled with delight. When they stopped spinning, she looked intently at the feather braided into Blake's long hair. Her blue eyes sparkled with mischief as she laughed and pulled at the braid. Blake smiled again as she squirmed to get back down. "Okay, okay! I'll let you down." As soon as her feet touched the ground, she picked up the wooden plate and headed back to Mistress Brewster.

"Good-bye for now. Let me know if you need help." Blake waved and walked away. His heart always melted when Humility was around. *Aunt Ann, she is doing so well.* Blake's eyes teared up. *I hope when, or if I get home again, I'm not so emotional. This could get very embarrassing.* He laughed out loud.

Captain Standish was setting up targets near the edge of the forest. "Let the games begin. We will see who has the greatest skill and accuracy with the musket." Standish shouted to the crowd. As Blake approached, he saw John and the other men loading their muskets nearby.

John called out to him. "Henry, are you shooting in the musket competition?"

"Squanto has taught me how to use the bow and arrow, but I have never shot the musket," Blake admitted.

"It is time you tried, my friend." John smiled as he passed the loaded musket. "Just take aim and shoot."

Blake took the long-barreled gun in his hands. He was nervous as he raised the musket to his shoulder, and peered down the metal barrel. His finger tightened slowly on the trigger.

Boom! The shot rang out as the recoil sent him backward. *Oh, no! I didn't even hit the target.*

Captain Standish patted him on the back. "Good try! I believe we need to set you up for more practice, Henry Samson!" Everyone laughed good-naturedly; it was all in good fun.

Blake laughed, too. "Sir, maybe I should stick to fishing and hunting with the bow and arrow!"

Blake handed the musket back to John and watched for hours as each participant took a turn, stood, and fired. There were two men left in the finals, one of them being Blake's friend, John. Whoever hit the final target would be the winner. Blake watched, silently cheering on his friend as John took aim at the target—and hit it!

"John Howland, you are the winner and master with the musket. Maybe I should enlist you in my militia!" Captain Standish shook his hand, and everyone clapped and dispersed. There was much gaiety and back-slapping as the men crossed the field.

Blake walked with John to the hilltop and they began setting up the foot-race contest. "Are you going to run in the race, John? You already won the musket challenge."

"You bet! We're running to the woods and back. Lizzy promised to come and watch. Remember our first race to the woods? It seems like such a long time ago. Are you going to race against me today?"

Before Blake could answer, he looked to the woods and saw Massasoit and many of his warriors riding out on horseback. There had to be 90 or more Pokanokets. Squanto hurried over to greet them, and Governor Bradford immediately met them in the field. It was an incredible sight.

Squanto translated the chief's words to Bradford. "Chief Massasoit heard all of the gunshots from the muskets. He thought you might be in trouble and came to your aid with his many brave warriors."

"Tell the Great Chief Massasoit we are thankful he and his brave warriors came to our aid," Bradford responded. "But rather than being in distress, we are having games and celebrating the great harvest that our God has provided. It would be a great honor if he and his mighty warriors celebrated with us, for this land gives life to both the English and the Pokanoket alike. We will be feasting for three days."

Once again, Squanto translated. Chief Massasoit nodded to Governor Bradford. "Our Mighty Chief has accepted your invitation. He and the warriors will now hunt game to bring to the celebration." As Squanto spoke the words of the Chief, he and his men turned and headed back into woods. Their horses' hooves sounded like the rumble of thunder until they were completely out of sight.

Within hours, Chief Massasoit and the warriors returned with five deer.

John turned to Blake. "In England, only rich people were allowed to shoot deer," he remembered. "This is a land of plenty. We have been blessed beyond measure."

More fires were set up as they prepared and roasted the deer on open spits. When the feast was ready, as was the custom, the servants and children ran back and forth bringing food to the guests and carrying platters of food and drinks of ale and spring water. Both the guests and the settlers ate much of their food with their hands, and then used a huge napkin to wipe their hands and faces clean.

Chief Massasoit and the Pokanoket sang and danced for the Pilgrims. They set up targets and demonstrated their skill using bows and arrows while riding bareback on their ponies. They competed at bouts of wrestling and jumping contests. At night, they camped in the field and continued burning fires and dancing long into the night. For three days, they feasted and celebrated. It was a joyous time, but after three days, it was time to return to the everyday duties and life at Plymouth Colony. In the company of all, Governor Bradford offered up a prayer of thanksgiving to officially end the celebration.

"Almighty God, it is with a heart filled with thankfulness that we end this time of celebration. Just as our ancestors celebrated your grace and provision at the Feast of Harvest, we also acknowledge and confess with great gladness, of the benefits and deliverances of God, both toward ourselves and others to the praise of your Name. Amen."

After the prayer, Chief Massasoit and his men returned to their village. All the Pilgrims were busy storing and preserving the extra food in the storehouse or involved in cleaning up. Nothing left over could be wasted. Blake was in the field, cleaning up from the three-day celebration. It looked like a storm might be brewing in the eastern sky. Lightning flickered off in the distance. He saw John Howland and Lizzy standing at the top of the hill looking out at the darkening sky. Blake missed spending time with John. Lizzy had lost both her parents during the winter sickness, and John took every opportunity to spend time with her.

Blake walked over to them. "It has been a wonderful but exhausting three-day celebration. I think I'm ready for life to be normal again." They both looked at him and laughed. John touched Lizzy's hand and smiled.

"Henry, I have asked Lizzy to marry me, and she has accepted. We wanted you to be the first to know. We will ask Governor Bradford for his blessing and set a date." Blake rushed to his friend and shook his hand, then turned to Lizzy. "Cousin Lizzy, I have known all along that someday you and John would be married." He gave her a big hug. "I will miss seeing you both."

"But Henry, we're not going anywhere." They both spoke at the same time. "We will see you every day!"

Blake laughed. "I don't know what I was thinking. You're not going anywhere, and I'm not going anywhere." *I can't believe I said that!* "Congratulations. I won't say a word until you're ready to announce it yourselves. I'll see you later." Blake walked back to the field, where he found Squanto waiting for him.

"I am leaving, my brother, to spend time with my people the Pokanoket, and hunt for food before winter. It will be here soon. The storehouse must be full before the first snowflake falls. I should return within six or seven days." Squanto reached out and grabbed Blake's hand in farewell. "Be safe, little brother, until my return."

Blake stood and watched as Squanto disappeared into the woods. He felt all alone. Pangs of homesickness stabbed him like a knife. "I wonder if I'll ever go home again?" he said aloud. At least he could tell the wind and it would be a secret. The wind picked up speed and howled back at him. He tried to stop, but its force pushed him closer to the woods. *It's getting dark and I need to get back to the colony*, Blake told himself. Back to the little houses that line the dirt road. *I will stop and see the Brewsters and say good night to Humility.*

The wind pushed even harder at his back. Dry leaves almost blinded him as they swirled around him, then spiraled into the sky. Suddenly, the wind dropped, and the air was still. He heard a gobble. There was a wild turkey! *No way!* Blake was surprised that any had survived after the great Thanksgiving feast, and headed toward the sound to catch sight of the wild bird. Squanto had taught him many ways to live and survive in the woods, so he wasn't afraid of venturing further away from the colony. The turkey led him deeper into the woods. Even though the leaves crunched beneath his feet, it didn't frighten the turkey away.

"I probably should go back before the storm comes." Once again, he spoke into the wind and it captured his words and carried them away. *Maybe the wind will carry my words back home. Back to the fields and pastures where Rosie and Ben love to run. Back to my family. Back to American History class with Mr. Wilson. I just want to go back!* He thought again about going back to the colony, but the turkey didn't seem in any rush, and truthfully, Blake wasn't, either.

I wonder if this turkey speaks my language? He laughed out loud. *I'm pretty good at turkey talk! Surely all turkeys speak the same language.* Blake tried it, but it didn't work. The turkey continued to lead him deeper into the woods.

Big drops of rain started to pelt him. Just ahead, he saw the hollowed trunk of a huge walnut tree. Blake started to sprint there to get out of the rain. The leaves were wet and slippery. He felt the coin slipping out of his pocket—it had come out of the leather pouch and was flying through the air. He caught it just as it was falling to the ground. A huge bolt of lightning cracked and lit up the sky. The tree shook from the thunder, and the world started to spin around and around, faster and faster. He didn't have time to think about anything except the pain in his ears. The last thing he saw were the leaves rising in the air as his knees hit the ground.

CHAPTER EIGHTEEN
THE REAWAKENING

B lake lay on the floor with his hands cupped around his ears. Finally, the ringing in his ears started to subside. As he dropped his arms and opened his eyes, the coin fell from his fingers and started rolling across the floor. *THE COIN!* He started chasing it on his hands and knees. It was rolling and picking up speed as it headed right for a huge crack between the floorboards.

"Got it!" He grabbed it just in time and looked around. His jaw dropped. "Home! I'm really home, I think." Blake pinched himself to see if he was dreaming. A sudden peace and exhilaration hit him at the same time. "Home! I'm really home!" Tears flooded his eyes, and he was suddenly afraid to move. "I just want to be home."

As he sat on the floor, he studied the coin in his hand. *How can I hold it in my hand right now and not be catapulted to another time and space? Is it the combination of the thunder and lightning and the coin?*

Blake vividly remembered the moment Aunt Ann had given him

the coin on Christmas morning, a gift from Henry's parents to remember them by.

"Blake! Blake! Are you okay?" He heard his father's voice calling for him, boots pounding the steps as he sprinted to the top. Quickly, Blake hid the coin in his pocket as his dad rounded the corner of the stairs.

"That lightning was so close!" Dad exclaimed. "It hit the tree on the other side of the arena. None of the animals were hurt, but it certainly scared us all. I think it took about 10 years off my life! Do I look older?" His dad laughed, then repeated his original question. "Are you okay?"

It felt so good to see and hear his dad again. He just sat on the floor and smiled. He wanted to just sit and take it all in—his dad's face and voice, the hayloft, everything. *I wish I could just freeze this moment in time forever.*

Finally, Blake spoke. "Everything seems a little strange. My ears were ringing, but they seem fine now. I feel a little dazed, like I've been someplace else." *If my dad only knew just how true that is! I've traveled into history for almost a year, yet it was just a split second in real time. I found the coin, then woke up on the Mayflower as my ancestor Henry Samson; lived with my Aunt Ann, Uncle Edward, and baby Humility; lived with the Pilgrims; helped build Plymouth Colony; and became best friends with John Howland and Squanto. How can I tell him about the First Thanksgiving and seeing Chief Massasoit? I could never tell it all. I experienced everything. It was real...wasn't it?*

"You do seem a little out of it!" Dad agreed. "You must have picked up a history bug working up here with all this old family stuff. It didn't take long for that bug to bite you. Or maybe it was some kind of rare turkey bug! Yes, I bet that's what it was. A rare turkey bug!"

They both laughed.

"You do know I speak fluent turkey!" Blake joked. "That's very rare, too. You're probably right, Dad! I think maybe I caught the history bug, too."

His dad reached down, grabbed his hand, and pulled him to his feet to give him a big bear hug. Blake didn't want the hug to ever end.

"I see you've made some progress up here. That's a neat old desk." Dad walked over and touched the wood. "It looks like it's handmade."

"It is, Dad. Look at the inscription: '*Peter James to Clara, my loving wife, March* 1820'. I'm using it to sort the papers that I find. When I'm finished, I'd like to keep it in my room. Will that be alright?"

"Well, ask your mother, but I bet she'll be thrilled that you want it. You might have caught her antique bug, too!"

"You better watch out. Sounds like a lot of bugs are going around!"

Dad laughed again. "I need to get back to the chores. Jackson and I have to cut up the limb that was struck by lightning. I think if you work on this project until lunch, you can be finished for today."

"Thanks, Dad. I promised Rosie we'd go for a ride."

After his father left, Blake took the coin out of his pocket and put it back into the secret drawer. He needed time to think about all that had happened to him after he found it. He felt changed—and he already missed the family he had left behind at Plymouth Colony. It didn't seem fair that he couldn't be both places at once. *Will Squanto notice a change in the real Henry? When will John and Lizzy get married? Will the real Henry Samson continue to love and care for Humility? So many questions. Will I ever have all the answers?*

There was still so much to do, but he looked forward to spending more time here in the future. *History really came alive here for me. And I want to find out more. More of everything. More about my ancestors, more about history—maybe even more about myself.*

At lunch time, before he headed down the stairs, he grabbed the old milking stool to surprise his mom.

It was so, so good to be home again! Blake's heart swelled with emotion. The storm had passed, and the air had a nice clean smell to it. He saw Dad and Jackson standing by the tree that had been struck by lightning. He wanted to just let the scene soak in. So many times, he had longed for this moment, and now he was back home, his wish come true. A smile danced on his lips.

"Will the tree live?" Blake asked, seeing the huge branch on the ground. Dad and Jackson had the chainsaw out and they were cutting it and stacking the pieces.

"We will have some nice firewood this winter!" Dad remarked. "As for the tree, I'll wait and see how it looks. It might just survive. I'm in no rush to cut it down."

Blake took a deep breath and inhaled the smell of the cut wood after the rain. It reminded him of his many times cutting firewood and stacking it outside in the rain with John Howland.

"Do you need some help? I can help you stack the wood."

"We did all the hard work, and now you want to come and help! Figures! I see you even brought your own stool to sit and watch!" Jackson gave his brother a big smile to show him he was joking.

"Sure, I knew you and Dad would want to have all the fun and I could sit on the stool and supervise you," Blake quipped, picking up a big handful of sawdust and stuffing it down the back of Jackson's shirt before he took off running to the house.

"And the stool is for Mom. It's a surprise."

"Blake! Now I'm gonna be all itchy!" Jackson took off his shirt and shook it in the wind. Blake could see the wet sawdust stuck to his back.

It is so good to be home!

After he washed up, he grabbed some lunch meat and cheese from the fridge and made three big sandwiches. He would take one each to Dad and Jackson. But first, he had a big glass of milk. *No more aqua vitae for me! Ha! Just good-old, cold milk.*

"Hi, Blake!" Mom walked in from the garden with a basketful of red tomatoes. "Want a fresh tomato to go with your sandwich?"

"Sure, Mom! And thank you for all the hard work you do in the garden. I appreciate all the good things you do for us, for our family. I don't know if I've ever told you that before."

She smiled at him. "Why, Blake, thank you! But you still have to organize the stuff in the loft!"

"Oh, Mom. I didn't say it to get out of work! I really mean it. And I want to organize the loft. There's a lot of interesting things up there. And there's an old desk that I would like to keep in my room, if that's all right. And look what I found for you. It's an old milking stool." He reached under the counter and handed her the milking stool he had hidden there.

"This is amazing!" She admired it, walked over to the wide shelf in the kitchen, and put it there. She placed an ivy plant on top. "This is so cute. Thanks for thinking of me. It fits perfectly." She gave him a big hug. "I think it's great that you want that desk in your room. It is a part of your family history. Just make sure you dust it *before* you bring it in the house." They both laughed.

"I think it would be fun if we planned another trail ride and camped out down at the river. Fall is the perfect time of year, and I've been hungry for hotdogs and s'mores cooked over an open fire. And we could all be together." Blake smiled at her.

"Sounds like a plan! Maybe we can go next weekend. I'll check with your father."

Blake heard the screen door slam behind her as she hurried back outside.

When he was finished eating, he walked out to the garden. Mom and the girls were busy. Layla was at the faucet using the hose to spray the mud off the vegetables before stacking them in a basket. He remembered the beautiful Pokanoket basket that Captain Standish had found buried in the sand with 36 ears of corn inside.

Annie was searching through the leaves, looking for pumpkins.

Blake loved teasing his sisters. "Did you know that after Squanto taught the Pilgrims how to plant crops that first spring at Plymouth Colony, then he just watched them. He said it was *'women's* work.' His job was to hunt and fish!"

"Well, I wish he was standing right here!" Annie said indignantly. "I'd tell him exactly what I thought about that!"

Blake laughed out loud. "I bet you would, Annie! A lot has changed since then. We learned in American History that cultures and roles were different then." He thought of Lizzy Tilley and how much she reminded him of Annie.

"Looks like you all are out here playing in the mud!" Blake laughed again as he greeted his mom and Layla.

"We have to get these vegetables picked before they rot on the vines, and I want to set the pumpkins on the porch. I have corn stalks to add for the fall decorations. And today's the only day to do it. So, yes, we're playing in the mud." Mom had a big streak of mud on her forehead.

"Blake, we are not playing. This is hard work!" Annie looked up with a big pumpkin in her hand. "Maybe you should help!"

"Sorry, Annie. I can't help! I have *men's* work to do." He laughed and ran as a big tomato came rocketing past his ear. "Mom let me know if you need my help later. I will be glad to play and work in the mud with you guys. It will be fun."

"Oh, we'll be sure and let you know!" They all laughed as he headed back to the kitchen. He grabbed the sandwiches he made for his dad and Jackson, along with a couple bags of their favorite chips, and walked back to where they were working.

CHAPTER NINETEEN
PROMISES REMEMBERED -
A PROMISE TO KEEP

Jackson was still working at the tree when Blake approached with his lunch. "Here's my peace offering."

"Thanks, Blake. I was getting pretty hungry, but I didn't want to stop until I finished here." He sat down on the log and started chewing the sandwich and munching the chips.

Blake found his dad in the barn sharpening the chain saw blade. "Here's a sandwich and chips. Made special. No bugs!" They laughed together. Blake sat with his dad on the bench until the sandwich was gone. He handed him a bottle of water from the cooler nearby.

"Can you help me get the desk to my room?" Blake asked. "Mom said it was all right if I kept it there, as long as I dust it *before* bringing it in the house."

"Yep, sounds exactly like your mom." They both chuckled.

"Now's a good time. Jackson has to finish stacking the wood

before I can cut more with the chain saw."

After dusting and polishing the desk with polish he found in the barn, they carried it down the barn steps and back to the house to his room. When his dad left, Blake opened the drawer and examined the hidden compartment. The coin was still there along with the folded paper. He gently closed the drawer, grabbed his laptop, and went down to the kitchen to use the internet.

I've got to find out what happened to my family and friends on the Mayflower.

First, he would look up Henry.

"Henry Samson Pilgrim" …search.

Henry Samson (c.1603-1685) was baptized in Henlow, co. Bedford, England on Jan. 15, 1604. Son of James Samson & his wife Martha (Cooper), a sister of Ann, wife of Edward Tilley. Henry was noted in his father's 1638 will and bequeathed five pounds.

Oh, good! His father did remember him even though they never saw each other again.

He married Ann Plummer on February 6, 1636. He was about 31 years old.

Who is Ann Plummer? I don't remember her on the Mayflower. Oh, it says they don't know when she arrived at the colony. They had nine children. NINE Children! Wow!

Henry served in the Plymouth government as an arbiter, a surveyor, a constable, and on a coroner's jury. In 1/1/1638, they were granted land next to Henry Howland.

Who is Henry Howland? Blake typed his name and hit the search key.

Henry Howland was a son of John Howland! It looks like they stayed good friends. Maybe they named their son Henry after Henry Samson. I'm very proud to be your descendant, Henry Samson!

It was exciting as Blake typed in each name. "John Howland Pilgrim"…search.

John Howland (1599-February 23, 1673) was a passenger on the *Mayflower* with the Separatists and other passengers when they left England to settle in Plymouth, Massachusetts. He was an indentured servant and, in later years, the executive assistant and personal secretary to Governor John Carver. He signed the *Mayflower* Compact and helped found Plymouth Colony. During his service to Governor Carver, Howland assisted in notable early business of the colony, such as the making of a treaty with the Native American Sachem Massasoit of the Wampanoag. He married Elizabeth (Lizzy) Tilley in 1623. They had 10 children.

I knew you and Lizzy would get married, John Howland, but wow—you had more children than Henry Samson. He only had nine!

Their direct descendants include notable figures such as U.S. presidents Franklin D. Roosevelt, George H. W. Bush, and George W. Bush.

John, I also see many other names among your descendants. Our entire

U. S. history is changed because you were rescued when you fell off the Mayflower. First ladies Edith Roosevelt and Barbara Bush. Alice Hathaway Lee Roosevelt, the first wife of Theodore Roosevelt, Former Governors Sarah Palin (Alaska) and Jeb Bush (Florida). I even see famous poets Ralph Waldo Emerson and Henry Wadsworth Longfellow. There are actors/actresses, a conductor and pianist, opera singer, music video director, and the list goes on and on. Thank you for being such a good friend. I wish I could have told you about the amazing journey I was on, but I think you would have thought it was because I fell and hit my head! Ha!

Aunt Ann was next. He could almost hear her. "Godspeed, Henry."

"Ann Tilley Pilgrim" ...search.

Ann (Agnes) Cooper Tilley (c.1585-1621) was baptized on Nov. 7, 1585 at Henlow, co. Bedford, England.

That's the same place Henry was baptized...that's so cool. They show a picture of the parish church. I hope I can go and see it someday.

She married Edward Tilley on June 20, 1614. Some of her ancestry can be traced back to the 11th century. She died sometime during the first winter at Plymouth. She and Edward had no children.

I won't forget you, Aunt Ann!

Blake had to stop for a moment. He was glad to be home, but the memories of his family and friends on the *Mayflower* and in Plymouth Colony stirred up mixed emotions. He felt a sudden emptiness. It was a longing to find something that was lost.

My life will never be the same. Joy and pain, together.

Blake continued. "Edward Tilley Pilgrim" ...search.

Edward Tilley (c.1588-1621) was baptized on May 27, 1588 at Henlow, co. Bedford, England. He was the son of Robert and Elizabeth Tilley. He was a signatory to the *Mayflower Compact* and died with his wife, Ann, the first winter in the New World.

Thank you, Uncle Edward. I did my best to keep my promise. After Aunt Ann died, baby Humility stayed with the Brewsters. She was happy there.

As he typed in her name, he could see her cute baby face and her bright blue eyes.

"Humility Cooper Pilgrim" ...search.

Humility Cooper (c. 1619-prior to 1651) of Leiden, Holland, traveled in 1620 on the voyage of the ship *Mayflower* as a one-year-old female child in the company of the Edward Tilley family. Although Edward Tilley and his wife, Ann, died the first winter in the New World, Humility survived to live her young life in Plymouth Colony, returning to England possibly in her teen years. Her fate in England is unknown.

It looks like you were about 30 years old when you died. Maybe I can find something about you if I go to England someday. You were a very sweet baby.

"Lizzy Tilley Pilgrim" ...search.

Elizabeth (Lizzy) Tilley (c. Aug. 1607-December 21, 1687) was baptized in Henlow, co. Bedford, England on August 30, 1607. Elizabeth Tilley traveled on the *Mayflower*, at the age of about 13, with her parents John and Joan (Hurst) Tilley. Her parents, and her aunt and uncle Edward and Agnes (Ann) Tilley, all died the first winter, leaving her orphaned in the New World. She soon married, about 1624 or 1625, a fellow *Mayflower* passenger John Howland. They raised a large family with 10 children, all of whom lived to adulthood and married. As a result, they likely have more descendants living today than any other *Mayflower* passengers.

I could always tell by the way you cared for baby Humility that you loved children. Ten children! You took care of all who needed you. Thank you.

I can't wait to find out what happened to Squanto.

"Squanto" …search.

Tisquantum (c. 1585 [+ or − 10 years]-late November 1622) was more commonly known as Squanto. He was a member of the Patuxet tribe and was best known for being an early liaison between the native populations in Southern New England and the *Mayflower* Pilgrims, who made their settlement at the site of Squanto's former summer village. Squanto was stolen by English explorer Thomas Hunt and taken to Spain in his younger years. He was among a number of captives bought by local monks who focused on their education and evangelization. He eventually traveled to England and from there returned to North America in 1619. He returned to his native village only to find that his tribe had been wiped out by an epidemic infection; Squanto was the last of the Patuxet. When the *Mayflower* landed in 1620, Squanto worked to broker peaceable relations between the Pilgrims and the local Pokanokets that lasted more than fifty years. He played a key role in their early meetings in March 1621, partly because he spoke English. He lived with the Pilgrims for 20 months acting as a translator, guide, and advisor. He introduced the settlers to the fur trade and taught them how to sow and fertilize native crops. As food shortages increased, Plymouth Colony Governor William Bradford relied on Squanto to pilot a ship of settlers on a trading expedition around Cape Cod and through dangerous shoals. During that voyage, Squanto contracted what Bradford called an "Indian fever." Bradford stayed with him for several days until he died, which Bradford described as a "great loss."

Blake had to stop after reading about Squanto. It saddened him to think his life with the Pilgrims had ended so soon. Then he remembered Squanto's words: "I was anxious to get back to Cape Cod Bay and find my family. When I came here, the sickness had taken all but two of this village, and now I am the only one left. My whole family, my wife, my children, my parents—all had been taken. I cannot say their names until I also climb the highest mountain and walk the road to the Creator of All Things."

Squanto, you taught me many things about being brave and the importance of trust, honor, strength, wisdom, power, and freedom. I was saddened to read of your illness and death today, even though it really happened so long ago. But then I remembered you are with your family and can finally speak their names. You walked the great road to the Creator of All Things! Thank you, my brother. I will always miss you.

When he was finished searching for information about the

Pilgrims, he just sat there for a moment, trying to absorb it all.

These are more than just empty words about a time in history. These people are real. This really happened, and I was there!

Blake's thoughts jumped to the paper he would write for Mr. Wilson.

The Life of the Brave and Amazing Pilgrims by Blake James. *That will be the title of my history paper for Mr. Wilson. I can write about the hardships and courage of our forefathers and the vital part they played in American History.*

Blake heard once again Mr. Wilson's words from history class on that eventful turkey day: "I want history to come alive for you, just as if you are standing alongside our nation's early European settlers. All of the freedoms we take for granted started in an unknown wilderness on November 9, 1620.The Pilgrims courageously chose to cross the Atlantic in a quest for religious freedom. Without their courage, where would we be today?"

Blake thought once again of John Howland's words, spoken when they had been in the hold of the *Mayflower*: "I pray someday someone will tell the true story no matter what the outcome will be."

I will do my best, John Howland, to honor your request! Maybe I'll even write a book about it someday. But I will save that for another day.

Finished! Blake took the stairs two at a time, back to his room. He sat at the desk and opened the drawer that held the mysterious coin. Holding it, he quickly looked out the window. There was no sign of a storm or lightning off in the distance. *Whew! No storms brewing. I'm not ready for another adventure yet.* He held it just a minute longer before putting it back where it had been waiting so long to be found.

Blake opened the center drawer. *This will be a perfect place to keep my laptop when I'm not using it.* Then he paused, taking a closer look inside. "What is this? It's an old journal."

Carefully he removed it from the drawer and placed it in the middle of the desktop. The pages fell open to an earmarked page. There, right in the center lay a fragile old feather...a very old, deteriorating feather.

"That can't be my eagle feather!" he said out loud. It looked so fragile that Blake was afraid to even breathe on it. "It is...it is! My eagle feather! I can't believe it found its way to me. The eagle feather that Squanto gave to me! It's really here." Blake tried to calm himself down. He pulled the journal closer and tried to read the faded words.

"This eagle feather was given to Henry Samson by Squanto at Plymouth Colony in 1621. It was a symbol of a special bond of brotherhood between the two." Blake just sat there, staring at the page. "It's true! There was...there still is...a special bond of brotherhood." Squanto's feather had found its way from Henry Samson, through the ages, to Blake James.

Blake's mind raced back to that moment, standing on the dirt floor of the little cottage with Squanto.

"We now are brothers." Squanto reached behind his head and

pulled out one of the feathers from his hair. "I give this to my young brother Henry Samson. Feathers may arrive unexpectedly, but not without purpose. I feel the wind has whispered in my ear that you are the owner the feather was searching for. The great feather of the eagle was intended for you. You must accept it and be thankful for this sign of high honor. Now you must live up to its powerful symbols."

It seemed the wind carried the message across the centuries, across the miles, across the room, and wrote its letter across the page of the old journal, saved by his ancestors who had valued and respected its message.

"The feather found its way back to me," Blake said slowly. "Not by accident. Not without purpose."

He placed the journal back in the drawer. There was room for both items in the old desk—for both the new laptop and the old journal. "The old ways and the new ways." Blake smiled.

Time to keep his promise.

As he walked down the path to the horse arena, Rosie came galloping over to see him. She was showing off. "Hey, girl, wanna go for a ride?" Blake grabbed the lead rope that was hanging on the fence and tied it around her neck as she rubbed her face on his. "I really missed you, girl!" He led her into the barn and brushed her till she shone like a copper penny.

When she was saddled, they started down the trail and into the woods. "Come on, girl, I've been waiting a long time for this. I've got lots to tell you."

She nickered at him.

"Well...I found this old coin in a secret compartment in the old desk in the hayloft and when I touched it, I woke up on the *Mayflower*...THE *MAYFLOWER*! No! First...I should tell you about the trouble I got into in American History class...you'll understand better about me waking up on the *Mayflower*.

"Well, there were these huge beetles outside on the window...the ones like we have here that the turkeys chase around. Did you know I speak fluent turkey? Ha! And the girl sitting behind me, Hannah, let out this bloodcurdling scream..."

As he rode, Blake's words were caught up like leaves and were carried away by the wind...

The End

First there were these huge beetles ... girl behind me let out a scream ... "I found this old coin in the hayloft ... Woke up on the Mayflower ... American History class ...

Blake's Family Tree

James Samson — Martha Cooper Samson

Henry Samson — Ann Plummer Samson

Peter James — Clara Matthias James

Josiah James — Susannah Draper James

George Charles James — Nancy Metcalf James

Charles James — Elizabeth Ross James

Chris James — Hannah Park James

Jackson James · Layla James · Blake James · Annie James

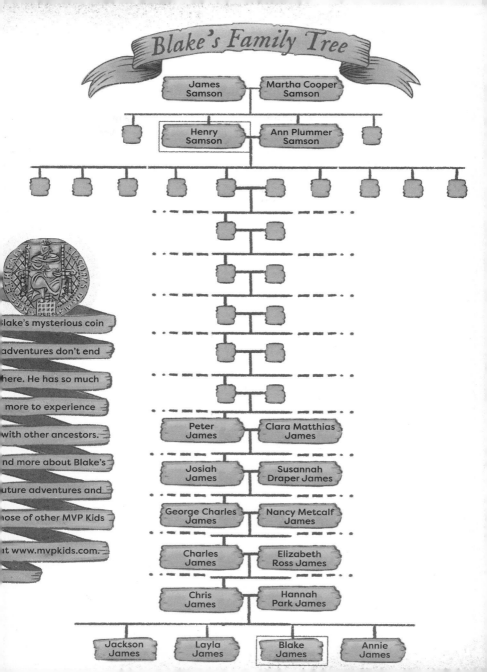

Blake's mysterious coin

adventures don't end

here. He has so much

more to experience

with other ancestors.

nd more about Blake's

uture adventures and

nose of other MVP Kids

t www.mvpkids.com.

Bibliography

PRIMARY SOURCE MATERIAL

The Pilgrim Chronicles, An Eyewitness History of the Pilgrims and the Founding of Plymouth County, by Rod Gragg (Regnery History, 2014)

ADDITIONAL SOURCE MATERIAL

The Boy Who Fell off the Mayflower, by P.J. Lynch (Candlewick Press, 2015)

Squanto's Journey, The Story of the First Thanksgiving, by Joseph Bruchac (Voyager Books, 2000)

Mayflower 1620, A New Look at a Pilgrim Voyage, by Plimoth Plantation with Peter Arenstam, John Kemp, and Catherine O'Neill Grace (National Geographic, 2003)

Pilgrim Hall Museum (www.pilgrimhall.org)

Mayflower History (www.mayflowerhistory.com)

Wikipedia

For additional resources,

visit our website at www.mvpkids.com.